# A CARNAGE BEFORE DAWN

BASED ON NIGERIA'S FIRST COUP D'ÉTAT

AYOMIDE AKINBODE

ISBN: 978-978-982-090-0



Published by:

Daneliherald Communications (Print Doctor Africa)
www.printdoctorafrica.com | 07030465088

## Author's Note

The events, names, and persons in this book are real. However, some of the conversations are fictitious, which might have never been said, due to the imagination of the writer. Therefore, the writer did not wish to malign any group of people or tribes who may find these conversations "uncomfortable".

Damola Awoyokun's exclusive article on the "First Nigerian Coup" published by The News Magazine in 2016 and Omoigui Nowamagbe's "SPECIAL BRANCH REPORT: "Military Rebellion of 15th January 1966" published on Gamji.com (Retrieved November 7, 2017) are my major sources for this novella.

– Ayomide Akinbode, Lagos, Nigeria.
  Monday, June 1, 2020.

In remembrance of Sergeant Daramola Oyegoke of the Nigerian Military Training College (NMTC) Kaduna, who was killed by Major P.C.K Nzeogwu for failing to shoot at the Northern Premier's Lodge in Kaduna, and to all those who were gruesomely murdered in the early hours of Saturday, January 15, 1966.

# Prologue

"Where's the master of the house?" Nzeogwu asked impatiently. Sensing the man could not understand English, he asked again in Hausa, *"Ina Sardauna*?

Where is the Sardauna?" Nzeogwu shouted, pointing his gun at the man who kept shaking his head asserting no knowledge of the Sardauna's location.

"If you won't tell me where your master is, I'll kill you," Nzeogwu screamed at him in Hausa.

"Okay, okay," the man replied fearfully and led Nzeogwu to the annex of the building. Three other soldiers followed Nzeogwu while Waribor and the rest returned to the staging area where the guns were manned.

As Nzeogwu approached the adjoining rooms the man was leading them to, he heard screams and cries of women and children.

"We will not allow you out there," the Sardauna's eldest wife, Hafsatu spoke defiantly.

"But I have to go. They are here for me not for you. You have to be strong. I have to go out there," the Sardauna pleaded. The other wives, with their children, were rattling their prayer beads in the midst of sobs.

As the Sardauna turned to go, Hafsatu held him firm in a tight embrace and wouldn't allow him to move. Zaruni, the Sardauna's head of guards came in and alerted the Premier that the soldiers were approaching the annex but promised to defend the family with his life and that of his men.

"Zaruni, I know you must do your duty but my safety is in God's hands," the Sardauna said.

"No, you can't die, you won't die," Hafsatu screamed in Hausa.

As she was crying, they heard gunshots outside. At this moment, Zaruni drew his bow and stood guard before the Sardauna and his family. With another sound of gunshots from his SMG, Nzeogwu kicked hard at the doors with his boots, which flung open and on sighting Zaruni, shot the poor guard who dropped dead at once, with his bow and arrows.

In the midst of the dark and screams of the women and children, Nzeogwu shouted, "Where's the Sardauna?" But the women would not allow him to move. Even the children were clinging to their mothers.

At last, the Premier managed to wriggle himself free from his wives but the eldest, Hafsatu, held on to him as he spoke.

"I am Ahmadu Bello, the Sardauna of Sokoto and the Premi…" With those words, Nzeogwu shot thrice at him; a bullet hitting his jaw, another at his wife,

Hafsatu, and the last one through his *babaringa* which penetrated his lower abdomen and lodged in his spinal cord.

The Sardauna and his wife fell with a loud thud to the screams of the women and children at the loudest decibels. It was music to Nzeogwu's ears. The mission had been accomplished. He had satisfied his blood lust and his enraged eyes were returning to their former calm state. He blew the whistle to signal the end of the mission. Operation Damisa had finally come to an end.

As Nzeogwu approached the gate, he met Waribor and his men of the Charlie Company.

"Did you get the man?" Waribor asked.

"Yes, I got him," Nzeogwu answered assuredly. He turned to the rest of the soldiers after he had got out of the gate and spoke triumphantly, "I have been successful, he's dead."

With that, they packed their remnants, got inside their Landrovers and proceeded to their next mission unchallenged leaving the Sardauna's residence in the glory of its former self. It was 2:45 am and the harshness of the harmattan had just begun.

# 1

# The Eve of Terror

***There is no terror in the bang, only in the anticipation of it.***

Sir Alfred Joseph Hitchcock, English film director and producer.

(August 13, 1899 – April 29, 1980)

***Friday, January 14, 1966. 7:45 pm***

***11, Thompson Avenue, Ikoyi, Lagos.***

"*As-salaam Alaikum,*" the voice greeted the figure who had his back to him but without a response. The voice then proceeded to tap the figure's left shoulder. The figure turned, startled at the sight before him, and threw a salute.

"Sir. I didn't know I was the one you greeted. Sorry, sir."

He waited for him to return his salute, but he did not. He had a smirk to his face, then he burst out in laughter. "Put down your hand, young man," he said in a heavy Kanuri accent, "Relax, everyone is in mufti here. You look frightened."

"Thank you, sir", I just feel nervous, that's all."

"I know. When an officer throws a salute in civilian clothes, it's more than nervousness," he grinned. "You can get a break if you want to. Unfortunately, the party is just starting, but I understand the stress you must have passed through for things to run smoothly."

"I'm fine sir."

"Okay then. See you around."

"Thank you, sir," he was about to throw a salute again, when he quickly remembered he was on mufti, then he stylishly scratched his head and walked towards the stewards.

Major Emmanuel Arinze Ifeajuna had lacked a good night's sleep for days and was thinking about how the events of the night would run when his boss, Brigadier Zakariya "Zak" Maimalari, the commander of the 2 Brigade Nigerian Army in Lagos, greeted him religiously, as a Muslim. Though he was a Christian, he was used to it and would always reply to his boss, but tonight was different. He was Chief-of-Staff to Maimalari and was in charge of his schedule and other related matters. Hence, he was the planner of the party and had sent invitations (in Maimalari's name) to the top hierarchy of the Nigerian Army. All senior officers with their ADCs (Aide-*de*-Camp) were there, including the GOC (General Officer Commanding) of the Army, Major-General Johnson "Ironside" Aguiyi-Ironsi, Colonel Kuru "Kur" Mohammed, acting Chief-of-Staff Army Headquarters, and Lieutenant-Colonel Yakubu "Jack" Gowon, who was to take over the 2nd battalion in Ikeja from the outgoing commander, Lieutenant-Colonel Hillary Njoku. They were all in mufti. Some politicians of the ruling party and cabinet ministers were there as well.

The party took place in Maimalari's home; the compound was a green sprawl patterned with stout palm trees and garden benches. Though it was during the Ramadan period, Maimalari did not concern himself too much with such rites. As the regimental orchestra performed, Maimalari joined the company of the GOC,

Gowon, and another senior officer. They were sitting on one of the garden benches under the palm trees. After some minutes, Gowon broke the ice.

"I have a bad feeling about the current happenings in the country," he said as he turned towards Maimalari.

"About?" Maimalari queried.

"The politicians may not know it," Gowon continued. Then he turned towards the GOC, "But Ironside sees danger and you can take it from me that he will never allow this country to be torn apart. The Federal Army is his pride and joy. His mastery of the nation's major languages intimidates me as a person."

"That's why we are soldiers and we should remain loyal to the government.And Jack, you should be able to speak Igbo by now. Your girlfriend, Edith, is Igbo." Ironsi spoke for the first and only time. Gowon smiled as he looked down bashfully.

"Then we need not conclude that the country is in danger," Maimalari quipped. "She's too young for that."

After the regimental orchestra had stopped, drummers and performers from the 2nd Battalion Headquarters in Ikeja filled the scene with a native piquancy. Maimalari used the occasion to show off his new fifteen-year-old wife from Kano and welcomed her to the South. Around eleven o'clock, all the senior officers left the party as well as the dancers, drummers, the servers, the orchestra, and the cleaners. To avoid suspicion, the junior officers then left one by one to dress up in full combat dress. Ifeajuna was the last to leave, being the busiest person that night. He had coordinated everything. Once he ensured everyone was done and left, he went to salute his boss who thanked him for a job well done.

No one had suspected that in a few hours' time, some of these junior officers who were drinking and joking with their senior officers would soon end the lives of some of them without mercy and turn Maimalari's new bride into a teenage widow. It was the eve of terror.

# 2

# The H-Hour

***The dog lives for the day, the hour, even the moment.***

Captain Robert Falcon Scott, British Naval officer and explorer.

(June 6, 1868 – March 29, 1912)

*Saturday, January 15, 1966. 1:10 am.*

*Ifeajuna's Residence, Apapa, Lagos.*

"Sorry gentlemen to have kept you waiting for such a long time. Accept my heartfelt apology," Major Ifeajuna said to the twelve officers of the Nigerian Army who had been waiting impatiently for him in his sitting room for the past two hours.

"We've been here since eleven last night," Major Humphrey Chukwuka, the Deputy Adjutant-General of the Nigerian Army, blurted. "You just kept us here waiting, doing nothing. Thank God for Rose who…."

"The man has apologised," Major Christian Anuforo, a General Staff Officer at the Headquarters, cut Chukwuka short. "Let's move on with the plan. Are we still on schedule? Ademoyega has sent the signal to the others that the H-hour is for two. That's…" He looked at his wristwatch, "Forty-seven minutes from now."

"What others? What's H-hour?" Captain Ganiyu Adeleke, one of the junior officers who was just recruited, queried. "What's this meeting for?"

The majors looked at Adeleke menacingly. "He needs to be filled in," they reasoned. Adeleke had not been part of the inner circle that was about to engage in bloodshed that would change the history of the nation. He had been "lured" to the meeting by Anuforo with the information that they were going, for "internal security operations", to Ibadan.

"Excuse me, everyone. Pardon my rudeness. The plan is still on schedule. But with respect to the junior officers here, let us state the objectives of our mission," Ifeajuna intervened.

"In light of recent events, especially with the senseless killings, lootings, and arson going on in the West which is threatening the peace of the Federal Territory here in Lagos, we think it is high time the Army took over power and put a stop to this nonsense," Ifeajuna stated. "If we pretend that all is well, then we are cowards. Because very soon, the wildfire that has started in the West will surely spread to other parts of the country which will eventually lead to chaos, disaster, and anarchy."

"Okay, let's pretend you are correct about the nation, shouldn't we inform our superiors?" Adeleke questioned.

"Like?" Anuforo snickered.

"Ironside, Maimalari, Colonel Mohammed, and other senior officers?"

"The only difference between them and the politicians is the uniforms they put on. They are birds of a feather. All of them are corrupt and have turned a blind eye to everything that is going on in the country," Ifeajuna retorted.

"Adeleke, listen well," Major Adewale Ademoyega spoke for the first time. "Our plan is to arrest the politicians and the senior officers and gather them at the Federal Guards Officers' Mess at Ikoyi, which will be our rallying point at the completion of our tasks and force them to resign and retire," he concluded.

"Ade is right," Chukwuka interrupted. "Once that is done, we form a new government. We release Chief Obafemi Awolowo from prison because we believe he's the one that can purge this nation and the parliament of its ineptness."

"And how do we hope to accomplish that with our superiors still alive?" Lieutenant Ezedigbo one of the junior officers questioned and continued, "Maimalari is in charge of the Brigade. How's that possible?"

"That's why we said you boys should calm down. The six of us had started the planning of this operation since August. As we speak, Nwobosi is on his way to Ibadan, Nzeogwu is in command at Kaduna, Obienu should be here soon before he proceeds to Abeokuta to get the firepower we need while Iledigbo and Agbogu will take charge of the operations in Benin-City and Enugu respectively," Ifeajuna said exultantly.

"But we won't reveal our plans further until we are assured of your loyalty," Major Donatus Okafor cut in.

"Yes, that's true," Ifeajuna said. "Do you agree with the plan? Are you for us or against us?" he asked. Everyone in the room agreed with the plan except Captain Adeleke who was still in doubt of their plans.

"I don't think it would be right for me to be part of this," Adeleke said reluctantly as he turned to leave the room.

"Captain," Ademoyega said sternly, "we know we may not be able to order you for this kind of operation but we need you and your soldiers. Also, we are trying to salvage a nation on the edge of a cliff. It is not for personal gains," he concluded softly.

"It's for the country," Captain Ogbonna Oji said.

"You are a stalwart. I know you well and your soldiers respect you for those principles you have always held on to. We won't force you but history will always favour those who do it right," Ademoyega implored.

"And if we are eventually successful, we may not be able to guarantee your safety," Anuforo threatened.

Captain Adeleke gazed at the floor, looked at Ademoyega, and then the other officers in the room whether he would see any ally that would support him but he found none, not even Lieutenant Oyewole, his fellow tribesman. He had no choice but to succumb.

"I'm in," he finally broke the silence.

"Good," Ifeajuna said, "let's proceed with the plan."

"It is important to note that anyone that is not with us is against us and may have to be taken out with extreme prejudice," Anuforo said.

"That's noted Chris, that's noted," Ifeajuna calmly cut him off. "Okay gentlemen, this is it."

While it was clear that everyone present was in support of the conspiracy, Ifeajuna, the head of the "revolution", issued the officers their different tasks and targets. The officers then roused their soldiers, the non-commissioned officers (NCOs), for the alleged "internal security operations", issued them arms and ammunition, and provided the necessary transportation through the Regimental Sergeant Major (RSM) James Ogbu of the Brigade Headquarters in Apapa.

With everything set in place and Mother Nature covering their tracks, they all rolled out fully kitted, convinced of a new Nigeria. To them, it was a revolution. A task that must be done. It was 2:00 am. It was the H-hour.

# 3

# Operation Damisa

***Men are more ready to repay an injury than a benefit, because gratitude is a burden and revenge, a pleasure.***

Publius Cornelius Tacitus, Roman Senator and historian.

(c.56 – c.120 AD)

*Saturday, January 15, 1966. 1:30 am.*

*Five miles from the residence of the Premier, Northern Region, Kaduna.*

For nearly fifteen days, residents of the Kaduna metropolis were already used to the nocturnalmovements by troops of the Nigerian Military Training College (NMTC) in Kaduna. Their instructor, Major Patrick Chukwuma Kaduna Nzeogwu had established these nightly military exercises that would eventually lead to the "Exercise Damisa" on the 13th and 14th of January, 1966. Ifeajuna had appointed Nzeogwu as the commander of the rebellion in the North but the manner in which it was to be organised was at Nzeogwu's discretion. Nzeogwu then went on to recruit Major Timothy Onwuatuegwu and Captain Gabriel Ude, both of the NMTC, and Captain Ben Gbulie of the Nigeria Army Engineers (NAE).

Camped in a bush about five miles, on Zaria Road, to the Premier of the Northern Region's (Sir Ahmadu Bello, the Sardauna of Sokoto) residence, was Nzeogwu with his soldiers. Some of them had no premonition of what was about to happen. They thought it was the regular night exercises they had been doing for the past fifteen days near the Ministers' quarters. Albeit, tonight was different. They were not near the quarters but a few miles to the Premier's residence. To their amazement, they had been armed with submachine guns, knives, grenades, torchlights, rocket launchers, and other military paraphernalia. Their commander, Major

Nzeogwu burned with fury as he spoke. His voice pierced the soundless and cold morning. His words bit through the harmattan's thick fog.

"Fellow comrades," Nzeogwu began. "Our long-term exercises have finally come to an end." The soldiers cringed at the word "comrades" but felt flattered to be addressed in such a way by their frightening commander and relieved to escape the parching and blistering cold winds.

"Nevertheless, there remains one last duty to be done," Nzeogwu continued. "A service to our country; *Operation Damisa*. As we all know, *Damisa* is the Hausa word for the leopard; an animal that is known to never change its spots. A perfect description of our corrupt politicians who are a symbol of filthiness through bribery, corruption, and nepotism. They are not ready to change and if we can't change them through the ballots, we shall, by God, change them through the bullets."

"This building," Nzeogwu continued, as he pointed to the Sardauna's residence, "is the realm of that filthiness and the Premier is the ruler of these corrupt subjects."

As Nzeogwu raged on about the Sardauna, how with his officials spent public funds on pilgrimages and unnecessary travels, the crisis in the West, and the Tiv riots, he also blamed the senior military officers who had romanticised themselves with the politicians and neglected their professionalism and duty to the nation.

"Gentlemen, this is the moment. The Nigerian Army is set to take over the reins of the leadership of this nation. I know this might have caught you by surprise, but history will always remember you for what you are about to embark upon tonight. The revolution is not just taking place here in Kaduna but it has commenced in Lagos and the regional capitals of Ibadan, Benin-City, and Enugu. You don't need to fear any repercussions because you are doing your duties as soldiers. You have the ammunition, instead of the blanks, so you can choose to kill me now and let the rot continue or you stand and march forward with me and rescue a nation we dream of for our children and their children's children."

He paused for reactions from them but no one flinched nor said a word. Who would dare at that moment? Nzeogwu had also said they were under orders which made them believe that the disobedience of a direct order from their superior would spell doom for them, although many of them were uncomfortable in raiding the Premier's residence on a cold night.

"I will take your silence as a 'yes' then." Nzeogwu finally broke the ice and proceeded with the laid-out plan. He brought out a blueprint of the Sardauna's residence and designated where every unit would stand and the roles they would play.

"Kpera," he called out to a Second-Lieutenant. "Give me your light." He then looked up and saw Onwuatuegwu in their midst. "Timothy, what in the heavens are you still here for?" He bellowed. "Proceed to your target and make no mistakes." Onwuatuegwu entered a Landrover with thirteen other soldiers and proceeded to the residence of Brigadier Samuel Ademulegun, the commander of the 1 Brigade Nigeria Army, Kaduna, for his task.

"Omeruah, Ude, stay with me. Waribor, gather your men. You are to eliminate the Colonel but abduct the Governor. I'll handle the Minister." Nzeogwu rolled out the orders. "Get me my transportation," he barked. Soon, a Landrover driven by a Sergeant arrived. It was loaded with ammunition. Twenty other soldiers followed in a convoy as they left for the Sardauna's Lodge.

On arrival at the Lodge, they met four police constables guarding the residence. They were alarmed when they saw the convoy but they stood their grounds. Nevertheless, their boldness thawed when they saw submachine guns pointing at them as the soldiers, led by Nzeogwu, approached them.

"Hands up, turn around, and face the wall," Nzeogwu ordered, raising his gun. One of them quickly complied but the three others were defiant. "*Kpruuuuuu, kpruuuuuu, kpruuuuuu*," Nzeogwu opened fire on them and the three constables laid dead instantly in a pool of their own blood. Some of Nzeogwu's men became terrified. The "revolution" had actually begun.

"Open the gates and load the ammo," Waribor ordered. "You, you, man the gates," he shouted at two soldiers from the Charlie Company of the 3rd Infantry Battalion. This battalion had questioned their boss Second-Lieutenant Dag Waribor why they had been given live ammunition instead of blanks for a routine exercise but Waribor told them it was for "internal security operations". This was the same challenge Gbulie faced with his engineers.

Captain Ben Gbulie was the deputy officer commanding the field engineers but he was at the time the commander of the 1st and 2nd Field Squadron, Nigeria Army Engineers (NAE) because his superior, Major Olusegun Obasanjo was in India for a course and had just arrived on that Friday morning of the planned coup but had not taken over command. Gbulie was the runabout agent for the night and could not go to the airport to pick Obasanjo. It was Nzeogwu, Obasanjo's roommate, who offered to pick him up. As expected, Nzeogwu kept him in the dark about the coup.

When Gbulie told his engineers about the operation that would require live ammunition, they questioned the legitimacy since the exercises had been over. But Gbulie, like Waribor, convinced them it was for "internal security operations". While distributing the tasks, Nzeogwu had told Gbulie to secure the Telephone Exchange, the Radio and Television House, State House, Ammunition Service Depot, and set up roadblocks on Kachia Road near the Police Barracks. In addition, Gbulie was also assigned the task of gathering some of the officers at the Headquarters for any support they might need.

"You are alright, sir," Ude told Nzeogwu who was still recovering from his latest shooting. Nzeogwu sniffed and continued screaming orders.

"Adebiyi, Manga, Oyegoke," he called out to his sergeants who were of the NMTC. "Load the Gustavs and set up the projectiles here." Oyegoke and Manga quickly got down with the projectiles, six in all, while Adebiyi was with the two 84mm Carl Gustav Anti-Tank guns.

Manga quickly loaded while Oyegoke crouched in fear as they set up the projectiles awaiting Nzeogwu's orders.

"Fire," Nzeogwu screamed.

But they fired timidly without hitting the main target nor giving the noise Nzeogwu wanted. Sensing danger, Adebiyi got down quickly to help Manga to reload while Oyegoke who didn't shoot at all was twitching with his weapon.

"Fire, you bastards, fire," he screamed again, this time approaching them with his SMG.

As Oyegoke sighted Nzeogwu coming towards them with his SMG, he made a quick dash for the dark. Enraged, Nzeogwu opened fire on the poor soldier and he slumped to the ground bleeding from multiple wounds until he gasped to his death.

"Adebiyi, take over Oyegoke's gun," Nzeogwu ordered. "And keep firing at the damn building," he screamed. Adebiyi kept on firing until the building caught fire.

Meanwhile, Waribor who had left to bring more men from the 3rd Battalion arrived with Omeruah and commanded the men to secure the outer wall of the Lodge and shoot anyone who attempted to leave the compound as there were screams of women and children emanating from the building and the scampering of civilians.

As the shooting was going on, a police patrol who had sighted the mutineers converging ominously in front of the Premier's Lodge radioed the British Police officer on duty at the Kaduna Police Operations room who in turn alerted Mallam Ahmed T. Ben-Musa, Sardauna's Senior Assistant Secretary (Security) through a phone call, who sprang up immediately and drove to the Lodge. As he approached the gate, the two soldiers guarding the gate showered bullets on him, killing him instantly.

It had been over fifteen minutes since the onslaught began, yet the main target, the Sardauna had not been found. Nzeogwu, Waribor, Omeruah, and fifteen other soldiers started conducting a room-to-room search. Corporal Yakubu Kaje, one of the soldiers who were at the rear, saw a silhouette of a figure, certainly a man, near the eastern entrance. Signaling to five other soldiers, they retrieved themselves from the group with the aim of capturing the unknown figure. The figure was tall and swift and seemed to know the compound well, judging by his movements.

"Hold it right there," one of the soldiers screamed. As the figure turned to the direction of the voice, he tried to draw his sword but the soldier shot to the ground and screamed again.

"Drop your weapon or drop dead." This time, he spoke in Hausa.

In the midst of the ensuing chaos, Major Nzeogwu arrived at the scene and asked the man the whereabouts of the Sardauna.

"Where's the master of the house?" Nzeogwu asked impatiently. Sensing the man could not understand English, he asked again in Hausa, "*Ina Sardauna*? Where is the Sardauna?" Nzeogwu shouted, pointing his gun at him but the man kept shaking his head asserting no knowledge of the Sardauna's location.

"If you won't tell me where your master is, I'll kill you," Nzeogwu screamed at him in Hausa.

"Okay, okay," the man replied fearfully and led Nzeogwu to the annex of the building. Three other soldiers followed Nzeogwu while Waribor and the rest returned to the staging area where the guns were manned.

As Nzeogwu approached the adjoining rooms the man was leading them to, he heard screams and cries of women and children.

"We will not allow you out there," the Sardauna's eldest wife, Hafsatu spoke defiantly.

"But I have to go. They are here for me not for you. You have to be strong. I have to go out there," the Sardauna pleaded. The other wives, with their children, were rattling their prayer beads in the midst of sobs.

As the Sardauna turned to go, Hafsatu held him firm in a tight embrace and wouldn't allow him to move. Zaruni, the Sardauna's head of guards came in and alerted the Premier that the soldiers were approaching the annex but promised to defend the family with his life and that of his men.

"Zaruni, I know you must do your duty but my safety is in God's hands," the Sardauna said.

"No, you can't die, you won't die," Hafsatu screamed in Hausa.

As she was crying, they heard gunshots outside. At this moment, Zaruni drew his bow and stood guard before the Sardauna and his family. With another sound of gunshots from his SMG, Nzeogwu kicked hard at the doors with his boots, which flung open and on sighting Zaruni, shot the poor guard who dropped dead at once, with his bow and arrows.

In the midst of the dark and screams of the women and children, Nzeogwu shouted, "Where's the Sardauna?" But the women would not allow him to move. Even the children were clinging to their mothers.

At last, the Premier managed to wriggle himself free from his wives but the eldest, Hafsatu, held on to him as he spoke.

"I am Ahmadu Bello, the Sardauna of Sokoto and the Premi…" With those words, Nzeogwu shot thrice at him; a bullet hit his jaw, another hit his wife, Hafsatu, and the last one into his *babaringa* which penetrated his lower abdomen and lodged in his spinal cord. The Sardauna and his wife fell with a loud thud to the screams of the women and children at the loudest decibels. It was music to Nzeogwu's ears. The mission had been accomplished. He had satisfied his blood lust and his enraged eyes were returning to their former calm state. He blew the whistle to signal the end of the mission. Operation Damisa had finally come to an end.

As he approached the gate, he met Waribor and his men of the Charlie Company.

"Did you get the man?" Waribor asked.

"Yes, I got him," Nzeogwu answered assuredly. He turned to the rest of the soldiers after he had got out of the gate and spoke triumphantly, "I have been successful, he's dead."

With that, they packed their remnants, got inside their Landrovers, and proceeded to their next mission unchallenged leaving the Sardauna's residence in the glory of its former self. It was 2:45 am and the harshness of the harmattan had just begun.

# 4

# A Cold Dawn in Hell

***Lord, protect me from my friends; I can take care of my enemies.***

François-Marie Arouet (Voltaire), French writer, historian, and philosopher.

(November 21, 1694 – May 30, 1778)

***Saturday January 15, 1966. 2:10 am***

***8, Ikoyi Crescent, Ikoyi, Lagos.***

*"Shhh,"* Chukwuka hushed at one of his men who was making a tapping noise with his footsteps as they crouched decidedly towards the building.

Major Chukwuka, together with Second-Lieutenant Godwin Onyefuru, and five other soldiers had been assigned the task of kidnapping and arresting the Adjutant-General of the Nigerian Army, Lieutenant-Colonel James Yakubu Pam, from his official residence. His wife, Elizabeth, and all other members of his family had just gone to bed a few hours ago. Pam was Chukwuka's superior and had always handed over the duties of his office to him anytime he (Pam) was not around. Ifeajuna needed Chukwuka for this assignment due to his position as the DAG, though he had been moderate in their revolutionary views as he was against any form of killing. It was nauseating to Ifeajuna but he needed him for the assignment.

As they approached the rear of the house, Chukwuka ordered two of the soldiers to stand guard and survey the premises. "Okibe, Ayanwu, stay here and watch out for hostiles. The rest of us will proceed," Chukwuka whispered. "Any resistance must be nonlethal. No killings. That's an order. Is that understood?"

"Yes sir."

"Good. Let's go."

When they got to the kitchen, they found the door locked. Suddenly, in a bit of rage, Onyefuru shot at the door and the soldiers trotted in hurriedly. By now, the whole household had woken up and was in trepidation. With a quick run up the stairs, the soldiers took over the bedrooms. Elizabeth was no longer in doubt that something had badly gone wrong. As she ran to the children's rooms in her anguish and confusion, she screamed for her eight-year-old eldest child and daughter.

"Kaneng! Kaneng! Help me! Help me!" she called out.

However, the invading soldiers had come face-to-face with her husband, led by a man very close to him and a family friend.

"Sir, we have come to take you with us," Chukwuka said.

"Why? What is the meaning of this?" Pam questioned.

"Sir, please come with us,"

"Ok. Allow me to dress up," Pam said as he gave in, especially to the sight of the guns glaring at him.

"Okay, sir. You have five minutes. Please, put on something thick. It's very cold outside."

At this point, Pam was joined by his heartbroken wife, Elizabeth, as he retreated into the bedroom and changed swiftly into a pair of trousers, a vest, and a shirt, and then put on his watch. After the five minutes had elapsed, Chukwuka knocked ferociously at the door to compel him that his time was up. Pam returned to the waiting soldiers as Elizabeth pleaded with Major Chukwuka, who she knew well as her husband's deputy and friend, to spare her husband's life.

"Please don't kill him, please don't kill my husband," Elizabeth pleaded.

"No. We won't Madam. Don't worry. I will bring him back to you," Chukwuka assured.

Major Chukwuka, who had rather become impatient, began to march the senior officer out of his home. As Pam was led out, Kaneng, his daughter, aware of the present danger, ran to her father and hugged him. Pam promptly turned to his wife and implored her to look after herself and the children. It was the last time he would have a glimpse of his family.

To the rendezvous," Chukwuka ordered Sergeant Iwueke who had been their driver as they proceeded to their rallying point.

Chukwuka heaved a sigh of relief. His assignment had been completed. There had been no killings. There had been no death. As for Pam, whose duties, until that morning, was to enlist new soldiers, saw to the payment of all soldiers and their promotion, looked after their discipline, welfare, medical care and even their discharge and burial in the case of death, he couldn't understand why his deputy would abuse his person and office by abducting him in the presence of his family. He remembered his wife and children and felt dejected. He dropped his head like a bat as the vehicle moved on stealthily. He had been warned about Chukwuka but he had argued that it would be a cold dawn in hell for Chukwuka to betray him. Indeed, it was, when Pam finally saw him in his home baring a gun to his face.

# 5

# The White Flag

**When I let go of what I am, I become what I might be.**

Lao Tzu, Chinese philosopher and writer.

(604 – 531 B.C.)

***Saturday, January 15, 1966. 2:40 am.***

***Residence of the Deputy Premier, Western Region, Ibadan.***

"Fani-Kayode! Come down, you are for lawful arrest by the army," Nwobosi shouted.

"I'm coming. I'm coming; don't shoot," a voice replied from a room upstairs, but there was no movement.

Nwobosi shouted again but there was still no movement. He then fired his gun into the ground as a warning. Yet, there was no sign of any movement. Nwobosi then ordered five of his men to follow him into the building. When they reached the door, it was locked as usual and Nwobosi was compelled to break a glass panel in the door with the butt of his gun and started ransacking the house despite being faced with three terrified children who were weeping uncontrollably as they hugged their mother in fear.

"*Shhh,* it's okay," Nwobosi told one of the weeping children, a five-year-old boy. "Where's your father," he asked. But the young boy shook his head in fright.

Eventually, Nwobosi proceeded to the bedroom with two of his men. As he kicked the door open, they were met by the sight of a frightened man with raised hands and a high-combed hair.

"I surrender. I surrender," the man said in fright, nearly weeping.

"Fani-Kayode, you have wasted a lot of time; we could have killed you. This is a lawful arrest by the army," Nwobosi countered.

"Please, don't kill me," Fani-Kayode begged.

"No, you're under arrest. Our orders are to bring you to Lagos."

Captain Emmanuel Nwobosi was the Commanding Officer, Field Artillery Battery in Abeokuta. He had been recruited by Ifeajuna three days before the "revolution" during the Brigade Training Conference in Lagos after Majors Alexander Madeibo and Mac Nzefili, the deputy commander of the 4th Battalion, Ibadan had turned down his request with the excuse that the coup might fail. Ifeajuna was disappointed, especially with Nzefili. He had been sure that Nzefili would easily be co-opted as he (Ifeajuna) had visited Ibadan regularly to discuss with him, though he met his wife most times. Nzefili's refusal was a big blow, he had the control of the second-largest battalion in the country, as his boss, Lieutenant-Colonel Abogo Lagerma would be in Lagos for the training. So, it was a relief for Ifeajuna when Nwobosi agreed to the operation, in the eleventh hour, at Ibadan, although he was unfamiliar with the city.

Around seven o'clock in the evening, Ifeajuna had signalled to Nwobosi that the H-hour was 0200 hours and should get his transportation and ammunition from the 2nd Recce Squadron in Abeokuta which was headed by Major John Obienu, who was also in Lagos and part of the plan but failed to show up on the morning of the "revolution". Ifeajuna had issued a forged order in Maimalari's name in case any senior officer challenged him or the quartermaster needed proof before the issuing of ammunition and written instructions containing the arrest of the Premier and Deputy Premier of the Western Region. Nwobosi ordered key NCOs of his unit for an "internal security operations" in Ibadan and then proceeded to the Squadron where he met Captain Remawa and Second-Lieutenant Orok with a message, purportedly from their boss, Obienu, on the need for transportation. They promised to provide the vehicles, a 3-Ton truck and a Landrover, with drivers by midnight.

Few minutes after midnight, Nwobosi woke up Second-Lieutenant Egbikor who was of his unit and Sergeant Ibolegbu whom he ordered to prepare all the unit's stock of small arms and ammunition for an immediate issue to the soldiers. With that done, the soldiers marched to the parade ground where they were addressed by Nwobosi who told them they were proceeding to Ibadan for "internal security operations". With a convoy of 16 Gunners, 2 Lance Bombardiers, 2 Sergeants, 1 Trooper, 1 Battery Quartermaster-Sergeant, 1 Second-Lieutenant, and 1 Captain in a 3-Ton truck and a Landrover, they moved off to Ibadan. While in Abeokuta, they met a pregnant woman in labour, wriggling in pains and Nwobosi ordered the Landrover driver, Trooper Itodo to stop. They assisted her and took her to the nearest hospital there in Abeokuta.

Thereafter, they proceeded without interruption until they reached Agodi, Ibadan around 2:15 am and headed straight to the Telephone Exchange building in Agodi. Nwobosi and Egbikor ordered all the employees to leave the building with the thought it would stop communication in and around Ibadan. Unlike Lagos, where the telephone exchange was partly automatic, Ibadan's exchange was fully automatic. Hence, asking the workers to go home did not silence the phones but continued working throughout the night.

Leaving the Telephone Exchange, they drove to the Electricity Corporation of Nigeria (ECN) at Eleyele where Nwobosi ordered the workers to halt all power generation and leave for their homes. Ibadan, already used to the darkness, was plunged into blackness. Some of the employees, who lived around the Dugbe axis of the city, prevailed on Nwobosi to give them a ride when he had asked for directions to the Premier and Deputy Premier's houses. Nwobosi was a gentle officer. He offered them a lift and they directed him to Fani-Kayode's residence.

When Nwobosi and his men arrived at the Deputy Premier's residence, the 3-Ton truck remained outside and as the Landrover drove into the compound, they were confronted by two policemen. As they overpowered one of them and bundled him into the Landrover, the other escaped. Entering the compound of the main residential building, Nwobosi and his men were shocked at the number of the armed thugs present there. But they were caught by surprise when the thugs quickly ran away when they sighted the armed soldiers. They had been ready for a battle and Nwobosi proceeded to shout Fani-Kayode's name.

"You are taking us to your boss' house," Nwobosi taunted Fani-Kayode as they tied him up with rifle slings in front of his wife and children.

"Please don't kill him," his wife pleaded.

"We won't if he behaves well and does what we require of him," Nwobosi replied.

"Please," the little boy whimpered with tears in his eyes. Nwobosi knelt down to him and promised his father's safe return. Thereafter, they tossed Fani-Kayode into the Landrover and proceeded to the Premier's house as he directed them.

In a flash, Fani-Kayode's wife dashed to the bedroom and picked up the telephone and dialled a number frantically. She was calling the Premier to report her husband's arrest.

*"Hello, who is there?"* Chief Samuel Ladoke Akintola, the Premier of the Western Region, spoke with a heavy Yoruba accent.

*"Baba…It's me, sir,"* the woman replied in the midst of sobs.

*"Ha, Adunni, what's the matter? Why the cries?"*

*"Some soldiers came here to arrest my husband. They may kill him. Please do something, sir."*

*"Soldiers? Ehen? You know what? Don't worry yourself, I'll handle this."*

*"You have to do something now, sir."*

*"I said I'll handle it. Let your mind be at rest. Your husband will be released first thing in the morning,"* Akintola assured and dropped the receiver. He reached for his phonebook and searched hurriedly for a number and dialed it. After some minutes, while attempting to dial another number, he heard noises from his courtyard. He looked out of his window and saw unfamiliar figures.

*"They are here,"* he said to himself and brought out his gun and cocked it. *"I'm ready for you."*

Nwobosi and his men had finally arrived at their destination. No thanks to the Premier's deputy who had easily raised the white flag.

# 6

# A First-Class Death

**Old soldiers never die; they just fade away.**

General Douglas MacArthur, American five-star general and Field Marshall of the Philippine Army.

(January 26, 1880 – April 5, 1964)

***Saturday, January 15, 1966. 2:10 am.***

***1, Kashim Ibrahim Road, Kaduna.***

"Timothy, how did you get in here and what the devil do you think you are doing?" Brigadier Samuel Ademulegun, Commanding Officer of the 1 Brigade Nigerian Army, Kaduna, asked bewilderedly as he saw Major Timothy Onwuatuegwu and five other soldiers pointing their submachine guns at him and his startled pregnant wife, Latifah, fondly called *Sisi Nurse.*

They had gained access to his bedroom having passed through with a little resistance from his guards commanded by Lance Corporal Lawrence Akuma and three sappers of the Nigerian Army Engineers. Immediately after Nzeogwu dispatched Onwuatuegwu for his task, he got into a Landrover with five of his men and headed for the Brigadier's house. On arrival, they met three guards; two on guard and one patrolling the ground. As he saw Onwuatuegwu and his men, he challenged them but he was easily disarmed and kept under guard with some of the soldiers.

Ademulegun was a much-disciplined officer and the second most-senior officer after the GOC, Aguiyi-Ironsi. His army number was NA4. He had joined the army as a Private in 1942 and was commissioned as a Lieutenant in 1949 and was the first indigenous Aide-*de*-Camp to the British Governor-General John Macpherson in 1952. He rose in the military ladder and became a Brigadier. As an officer of that magnitude, he was the most protected personality in the whole of Northern Nigeria. Even more protected than the Premier and Governor of the Northern Region. His guards, drawn from the 3rd Infantry Battalion in Kaduna, guarded not only the inside and outside of his compound but his main house too. But the guards had been compromised and had led Onwuatuegwu straight into the Brigadier's bedroom where he was just in his white singlet and knickers.

"Get dressed and come with us, sir. Those are my instructions – to bring you to the headquarters," Onwuatuegwu said to the Brigadier.

“What nonsense is that? Are you all out of your minds?” Ademulegun shouted at them.

“I’m only following orders, sir. Please, just do as I say.”

“Timothy, are you giving me orders?”

“As of this moment, yes, sir. We are out of time,” Onwuatuegwu replied impatiently.

It sounded like gibberish to him. As the commander of that headquarters since 1964, he was the only one who could give such an order. But all the while, his wife Latifah, eight months pregnant, planted herself fearlessly between her husband and the pointed guns. In the top bedside drawer was a service pistol. As a Brigadier, Ademulegun knew a pistol was no match for six soldiers armed with submachine guns. But he would rather fight and die gallantly than degrade the honour of his office by surrendering to subordinates.

"Alright then," Ademulegun said resignedly and made to get up from his bed.

But as he made a quick dash for the drawer to pick up his pistol, Onwuatuegwu opened fire on the Brigadier, his wife, Latifah, and the unborn child. Ademulegun's children, Kole and Solape who were in the next room, heard all the clash and were the first to see their lifeless parents surrounded by a pool of blood. Quickly, they dashed to the servants' quarters where they stayed till morning. Onwuatuegwu and his men then proceeded to their next mission blatantly as they left a sight too gory to behold, of his Brigadier and his wife.

*Hundred metres to Colonel Raphael Shodeinde's Residence, Kaduna. 3:15 am.*

"Timothy, what kept you so long?" Nzeogwu quizzed Onwuatuegwu who had just arrived near the Colonel's residence.

"We just abducted the governor. He's under guard at the headquarters. Besides, it was not easy convincing the Brigadier's security personnel but he has been *deleted,*" Timothy replied and then added dejectedly, "together with his wife."

Nzeogwu who looked relieved at first, on hearing of the Brigadier's death, now felt troubled.

"Sisi Nurse was pregnant. Tim, how did you involve her in this?"

"It was collateral damage. She wouldn't leave her husband and we were running out of time. That was the only solution. It was regrettable but it had to be done. What's done is done," Onwuatuegwu replied unemotionally.

When Nzeogwu himself remembered how he had gunned down the Sardauna and his wife a few minutes earlier, he regained his composure.

"How about the children?"

"They should be fine. We never saw them. Look, are we going to finish off with the plan or you'll continue interrogating me while we lose our next target?"

Nzeogwu knew that the death of Ademulegun was vital to the success of the "revolution", hence, his relief. However, he was fond of Sisi Nurse, she would always prepare him pounded yam with *egusi* soup and *bokoto* anytime he came visiting. He would carry her children on his shoulders and fling them around as well. They were fond of him and other junior officers who visited their home. They called them "Uncle" but Onwuatuegwu and his men murdered sleep when they emptied their bullets into their parents' bodies.

"Okay, fine," Nzeogwu said reluctantly.

"Sir, we are ready, Lieutenant Nwokedi interrupted them.

"Where's Waribor? He was supposed to be here according to the plan," Onwuatuegwu asked.

"He should be here soon. We were at Makaman Bida's place, but the old man has run away to his village. Waribor mistakenly killed his driver," Nzeogwu retorted.

"Sir?" Nwokedi called Nzeogwu with a voice of concern, "You are bleeding, sir. Right there at your neck."

Nzeogwu touched the wounded area. It was bloody. He had been wounded during his encounter with the Sardauna's bodyguards. One of them must have slashed him with a weapon but he couldn't remember when. He called for a bandage. He wiped the right side of his face and then he wrapped his neck with it. This made him angrier as he proceeded to the Colonel's residence.

"Colonel Raphael Shodeinde, you are under arrest by the Revolution High Command, sir. Step outside with your hands up," Nzeogwu shouted.

He did this twice but there was no response. As he was about to move in with his soldiers, suddenly, the security lights and interior lights were switched on from the inside. It was the Colonel's wife. She had been awoken by Nzeogwu's summons but the Colonel himself was still fast asleep. It was a deep sleep. A sleep unto the death. At once, Nzeogwu and his men opened fire and started blazing at doors and windows of the house with their submachine guns. Two bullets penetrated her left hand as she screamed, shouted, and screeched. Onwuatuegwu kicked the door open as Nzeogwu followed, then Nwokedi, and eight other soldiers.

"Please, don't kill me," Mrs. Shodeinde pleaded as she shrieked.

"Believe me, Madam, we are not here for you," Nzeogwu said assuredly.

"Where's your husband?" Onwuatuegwu shouted at her.

"In the bedroom," she quickly replied. As they approached the room, she begged as she kept on shouting.

"Raphael! Please don't harm him. What do you people want? Please don't......Raphael!"

To keep her from screaming, Nwokedi shot twice at her legs. She whimpered, made a quick limping dash for the door and escaped, for her dear life, to the servants' quarters.

By this time, the Colonel had woken up and was sitting up on the bed, clearing his eyes, when Nzeogwu and the rest of his men charged into the bedroom menacingly. Before the Colonel could utter a word, Nzeogwu and Onwuatuegwu opened fire and razed his body with bullets. Nwokedi and five other soldiers joined in as the

Colonel rolled off the sheets and fell down dead in a pool of blood by his bed.

Kaduna Nzeogwu and the rest of his men then left for the Brigade Headquarters contented with their successful mission. An epic but a bloody massacre. They had satisfied their driving belief. A belief which convinced them to murder their superiors in their beds without any iota of mercy. Now in total control of the North, the major awaited news from the South. He had completed his own part of the rebellion. Colonel Raphael Shodeinde was the Deputy Commandant of the Nigerian Defence Academy in Kaduna. He was the one Brigadier Ademulegun usually handed over the Brigade to whenever he was not around. However, Ademulegun and Shodeinde did not die as cowards. Both of them were "first-class" officers who died a "first-class" death.

# 7

# While Men Slept

**The enemy advances, we retreat; the enemy camps, we harass; the enemy tires, we attack; the enemy retreats, we pursue.**

Mao Zedong, Chinese Communist leader and the principal founder of the People's Republic of China.

(December 26, 1893 – September 9, 1976)

*Saturday January 15, 1966. 2:30 am.*

***Residences of the Prime Minister and Finance Minister, Onikan, Lagos.***

After Ifeajuna had dispersed his fellow mutineers with their tasks and targets, he, in turn, gathered his men in a convoy, with his red Mercedes Benz afore, and advanced to the Onikan roundabout; a few meters from the residences of the Prime Minister, Sir Abubakar Tafawa Balewa and the Finance Minister, Chief Festus Okotie-Eboh. Among the Revolution High Command in the South, Ifeajuna held the largest unit which comprised of twenty soldiers and two officers.

"Everybody, come down," Ifeajuna ordered. He then divided the unit into three groups with the officers in command.

"Ezedigbo, you are to arrest Okotie-Eboh with these eight men," Ifeajuna called out the names of the soldiers to the Second-Lieutenant.

"Onyeacha, you and these soldiers," Ifeajuna indicated each of them, "are on guard over the vehicles and the approaching roads. You are to stop and turn back any vehicle approaching this road. We don't want any interference."

"Yes, sir," the Warrant Officer saluted.

"Lieutenant," Ifeajuna called out to Second-Lieutenant Fola Oyewole. "You and I, with these soldiers, will take care of the Prime Minister."

"Yes, sir," Oyewole replied.

"Alright, let's move."

Ifeajuna and Ezedigbo both left for their respective targets with their men while Onyeacha maintained guard over the roundabout and the approaching roads and ensured that no vehicle entered or exited during the operation.

The Prime Minister, Sir Abubakar Tafawa Balewa, was a pious man and he hardly surrounded himself with guards at home or even when travelling. Ifeajuna knew his task would be easy, so he didn't recruit combat soldiers to carry out the arrest of the Prime Minister's arrest. They were service soldiers.

"*Gbam, gbam, gbam,*" Ifeajuna knocked fiercely at the gate.

"Who goes there?" A voice asked angrily from the inside. It was a Police Constable who was on guard within the premises.

"We are men of the Nigerian Army from the Brigade Headquarters," Ifeajuna responded. "We are under orders for added protection of the Prime Minister," he continued.

"Okay. But, *walahi,* at this time? *Oga* is already asleep," the policeman said as he opened the gate for them.

"That's why we are here. We are supposed to be on guard while noblemen slept," Ifeajuna replied to him sneeringly as he entered with the rest of his men. "How many guards are on ground?"

"Six, excluding me."

"Good. Show us where they are and handover your rifle," Ifeajuna ordered him sternly. He collected the rifle from him and passed it on to Sergeant Odunze.

When they got to the back of the house, they found the other members of the guard.

"Alright, everyone, hands up and surrender your rifles," Ifeajuna ordered them as the rest of the soldiers raised their submachine guns and cocked them. Five of them quickly handed over their rifles in fear.

"I said, hand over your rifle," Ifeajuna shouted at the last member of the guard who was with a patrol dog that was barking ferociously. In the midst of the confusion, Sergeant Odunze closed up to him, hit him with a blow on his face, and then disarmed him. He surrendered with a yelp.

"Iberesi, Okoh, Onwuli," Ifeajuna called out the soldiers' names, "escort them to the main gate and stand guard. You are to shoot anyone who tries to escape or raise an alarm."

"Yes, sir," they chorused.

Major Ifeajuna and the rest of his men then approached the rear entrance to the Prime Minister's residence having arrested the stewards. They broke into the lounge and the Major proceeded to the Prime Minister's bedroom.

"Who's there?" A voice queried from inside. However, Ifeajuna replied by kicking the doors open with his boots.

"You're under arrest, sir," Ifeajuna saluted and then pointed his gun at the Prime Minister, who looked startled. "Get up, we don't have a lot of time, sir."

"Alright," the Prime Minister replied gently, "allow me to dress up and pray."

After saying his prayers, Tafawa Balewa put on a white flowing robe with white trousers, a pair of slippers, and his prayer beads. Without fear and a disciplined face, he trudged out of the room and the residence gently as Ifeajuna and his soldiers accompanied him with pointed guns. When they reached the parked vehicles, Ezedigbo had arrested the Finance Minister, Chief Okotie-Eboh, and had tossed him like a bag of groundnuts into the back of the 3-Ton truck while the Prime Minister was assisted into the backseat of Ifeajuna's luxurious car, a red Mercedes Benz, as the convoy drove off to the rendezvous.

Major Chris Anuforo, a General Staff Officer at the Army Headquarters, aided by Second-Lieutenant Ngwuluka and six other soldiers proceeded in their two private cars to 1, Park Lane Apapa, the residence of Colonel Kur Mohammed who was the acting Chief-of-Staff at the Army Headquarters. The house was then being guarded by unarmed nursing orderlies of a Field Ambulance located in Apapa.

"Everyone, get down," Anuforo ordered all his men to alight from the cars, which had stopped some distance from the house. Afterward, they advanced towards the house led by Anuforo.

"Yes? Hold it right there," one of the guards challenged them.

"Shut up! Hands up," Anuforo screamed at him. He then ordered one of the armed soldiers to round him up and the other three members of the guard and watch over them.

*"Kho, kho, kho,"* Anuforo knocked at the front door impatiently. There was no answer. He knocked again.

"Who's there?" A faint voice asked from the house.

"Why don't you come out in the first place and see who is knocking?" Anuforo shouted. But there was no response. No movement from the inside. He knocked again, yet no answer. At this juncture, Anuforo ordered his men to cock their guns. He then kicked at the door, which swung open, and entered, accompanied by three soldiers.

They started searching the house hurriedly until the Colonel was found, in his pyjamas, in one of the bedrooms.

Anuforo ordered the Colonel out of the house who did not resist arrest. They had not allowed him to change into something more comforting despite the cold and harsh weather. Anuforo tied the Colonel's wrists with a rifle sling and together with the other soldiers, to one of the cars,they drove off to their next target.

Anuforo's next target was the residence of the Quartermaster-General at the Army Headquarters, Lieutenant-Colonel Arthur Chinyelu Unegbe. His house at 7, Point Road, Apapa, was just a few metres away from Colonel Mohammed's house. So, Anuforo ordered some of the soldiers to follow on foot due to the presence of the Colonel in the car.

As the Quartermaster-General, Lieutenant-Colonel Unegbe was responsible for the provision of every weapon, ammunition, vehicle, equipment, clothing, and food for the Army in general. Although he held no command nor battalion of troops, he was a senior officer who, as a threat to the "revolution", had to be gunned down. Without the death of the senior officers, their "revolution" stood no chance.

On arrival at Unegbe's house, Anuforo entered alone. When he found him, he shot him immediately in the presence of his pregnant wife. Anuforo came downstairs and ordered some of the soldiers to bring out the dead body of the Lieutenant-Colonel.

"Come down from the car, sir," Anuforo called out to Colonel Mohammed calmly who got down and stared hard at him. The Colonel had not spoken a word since his arrest and the cold did not help matters at all. Still tied with the rifle slings, he had expected the worst.

"Say your last prayers, sir," Anuforo said, "you are to be shot."

Colonel Kur Mohammed glared but did not plead for mercy nor argue in any other manner. Like a zephyr, he was gentle and calm as he simply knelt down and mumbled a silent prayer until he was rained, in the back, with bullets by Anuforo who had been restless with his gun for the past one hour. The Colonel fell face-down as life hissed out of him.

Colonel Mohammed's body was then crammed into the boot of Anuforo's car while Unegbe's body was placed on the floor at the back of the car. The vehicles then proceeded to the Federal Guard Officers' Mess where he met Major Chukwuka and his unit with the Adjutant-General at the Army Headquarters, Lieutenant-Colonel James Yakubu Pam, who had been waiting at the rendezvous for the rest of them. At the Mess, the two bodies of Colonel Mohammed and Lieutenant-Colonel Arthur Unegbe were unloaded on the ground. It was 3:10 am.

Brigadier Zakariya Maimalari, the Commander of the 2 Brigade, Lagos, had just woken upto pick his phone, that had been ringing, at his 11, Thompson Avenue, Ikoyi, home in Lagos around 2:00 am, where a cocktail party had just ended a few hours earlier. It was Elizabeth, the wife of Lieutenant-Colonel James Yakubu Pam, who was calling to apprise Maimalari of what had happened earlier at their residence and how some soldiers had gained forceful entry into their bedroom to arrest her husband.

Maimalari had hardly spoken to Mrs. Pam when he himself heard gunshots at his own gate. Maimalari's guard commander who had adamantly denied the mutineers entrance to the residence had just been shot dead.

Immediately Maimalari heard the gunshots, he dropped the phone, ran upstairs to pick up his teenage wife, and kept her at the servants' quarters. He scaled the tall fence and disappeared into the darkness.

Major Donatus Okafor, the officer commanding the Federal Guards was tasked with the assassination of Maimalari. It was important Maimalari was cold dead if their revolution was to succeed. As Commander of the Southern Brigade in Apapa, Maimalari had under him all the fighting forces of the battalions, the field artillery corps, and the armoured and mechanised squads. He could effectively mobilise the entire brigade even if the country was suddenly attacked by a neighbouring army.

When Okafor realised Maimalari had fled the house, he became very annoyed. He ordered his men to search the compound and shoot the Brigadier on sight; he was not to be given any opportunity to capitulate. Without Maimalari dead, they were doomed. They knew their actions were high treason that carried the death penalty. Therefore, they had to be successful or die trying. Okafor then jumped into his vehicle driven by one of his soldiers and desperately searched around Thompson Avenue, Brown Street, and Glover Road, even all the way to Bourdillon Road.

Maimalari who had been hiding and running was trying to make his way to the Federal Guards barracks in his pyjamas when he heard and saw the light of an oncoming vehicle. He ducked into the shrubs again thinking it was Okafor and his men. Instead, he undoubtedly recognised the red Mercedes Benz which belonged to his Chief-of-Staff and Brigade Major, Major Emmanuel Arinze Ifeajunawho was transporting the Finance Minister and the Prime Minister to the Mess.

It was not immediately clear to Maimalari that Ifeajuna was part of the mutineers. Instead, Maimalari saw Ifeajuna as his hope and dashed for him. Ifeajuna ordered his driver to stop and he got out of the car with Ezedigbo, both of them armed.

"Emma, thank God," the Brigadier said with a look of relief, "some of the boys have gone crazy. They just attacked me in my home. Do you have any knowledge of who they might be and which unit?" He said with a taint of confidence he just found at the sight of his Brigade Major.

"No, sir," Ifeajuna replied with disdain.

"Never mind, just get me to the barracks. I'm going to find those bastards and finish them in the morning," Maimalari said as he ambled towards the car. Suddenly, he stopped short and caught the sight of the Prime Minister, seated in a draped fashion in the car, whose white clothing had made him conspicuous to the Brigadier.

Maimalari looked at Ifeajuna perplexedly. His throat dried up. He couldn't find the right words. He knew he had walked into a trap. He had escaped Okafor and his men but now found himself willingly in the tiger's den.

"Say your last prayers, sir," Ifeajuna broke the silence and cocked his gun. Maimalari just stared hard. Without warning, the Major fired three shots from his gun at the Brigadier, as one of the bullets ricocheted and hit Ezedigbo at the jugular. The young Lieutenant started bleeding profusely. The Brigadier's heartbeat stopped and he fell. This did not deter Ifeajuna. He fired five more shots to affirm the Brigadier's death. Once confirmed dead, his body was loaded into the 3-Ton truck with the tied Okotie-Eboh. Ifeajuna, who still had the Prime Minister in his car, then proceeded to the Mess with Ezedigbo still bleeding without remedy.

"Humphrey, why is Pam still alive?" Anuforo asked Chukwuka with a surprised look on his face as he saw the Lieutenant-Colonel with his head bowed in the Landrover which was at the Mess. Chukwuka had been waiting for others anticipating the next point of action.

"He was gentle. He did not resist arrest," Chukwuka replied calmly.

"*Ehen?* So was Colonel Mohammed. He did not resist arrest and now he's dead."

"I promised his wife that I would keep him safe."

"I don't care what you promised his wife. He's a senior officer. He has to die. Finish what you started. The revolution comes first."

"I won't kill him," Chukwuka replied defiantly.

Anuforo was furious as he made a move for the Landrover with his cocked gun.

"Chris, what are you doing?" Chukwuka asked, looking worried. "Christian," he screamed his name again.

But Anuforo ignored him and screamed at the driver to drive. With four other soldiers and Pam, Anuforo coursed through into the vehicle as it racketed towards Ikoyi, contaminating the calm night with its noises and fumes.

"Hold it right there," Major Anuforo screamed at the driver as he slammed at the brakes. He had found a grassy location in downtown Ikoyi far from the Federal Guard Unit, Dodan barracks. He didn't want any hindrances to the sinister action he was about to perform.

"Get out of the vehicle, sir," Anuforo ordered the senior officer after he had already alighted from it. James Pam got out gently from the Landrover in trepidation of what was about to happen next.

"You are to be shot sir and it would do well for you to say your last prayers," Anuforo said sternly after they had walked some few meters away from the vehicle.

"Chris, why?" Pam asked innocently as he turned facing him.

"I'm acting under orders, sir," the Major replied him scornfully.

"Chris, don't do this, please," Pam softly pleaded. "I have six young children to take care of. Please!"

"Sir, are you going to say your last prayers or not?" Anuforo asked with anger as he raised his gun.

Pam knelt down resignedly in front of him and prayed, "Lord save them. Lord bless them. Lord keep them." He rendered his last prayers, which were obviously for his wife and children.

In a blaze, without warning, Major Anuforo fired a burst from his submachine gun into the Lieutenant-Colonel's body. A plethora of bullets penetrated through, hitting his chest and jaw. The 32-year-old army officer fell as the cold, damp grass embraced him in a pool of his own blood. The soldiers who were in the Landrover watched in astonishment. They could not fathom why the Adjutant General of the Army on whose shoulders the responsibility of the welfare of every soldier rested until an hour ago, would just be so swiftly executed. It was in their presence that the Lieutenant-Colonel had asked his children to stop crying and had also told his wife to look after and take care of them that he would soon be back. Was this the "internal security operations" they had been awoken for? They were still meditating on these thoughts when Anuforo shouted at them.

"Are you all deaf? I said you should load the body into the vehicle."

Anuforo had ordered them at first but they were absentminded as to what he must have said before he repeated himself. The Major then pointed his smoking gun at them and shouted,

"Or, do you want me to waste you all?"

The soldiers, looking frightened, quickly got down from the Landrover and loaded Pam's body into the vehicle without a word. With the exception of Aguiyi-Ironsi, the GOC, the annihilation of senior officers, present in Lagos, in the top command of the Nigerian Army Headquarters had been accomplished. They all drove back to the Mess where the body was unloaded and placed together with the bodies of Colonel Kur Mohammed and Lieutenant Colonel-Arthur Unegbe.

When Ifeajuna got to the Mess, after he had killed Brigadier Zakariya Maimalari, Anuforo and Chukwuka were nowhere to be found. With time running out and not giving anything to chance, he, therefore, decided to take up Anuforo's task of eliminating all the battalion commanders of the Southern Brigade who were lodged at the Ikoyi Hotel. The commanders had attended the Brigade Training Conference in Apapa and were at Maimalari's cocktail party a few hours ago. The commanders, Lieutenant-Colonel Aborgo Largema of the 4th Battalion, Ibadan, and Lieutenant-Colonel David Akpode Ejoor of the 1st Battalion Enugu, were lodged in Rooms 115 and 17 respectively. But Ifeajuna did not know where they were lodged so he proceeded to the reception.

"How can we help you, sir?" A male receptionist asked the Major courteously.

"Yes. We seek our commanders. There's been a situation and they are needed as soon as possible," Ifeajuna answered him deceptively. He still had the wounded Ezedigbo, whose bleeding had subsided, and the Prime Minister in his red Mercedes Benz.

"Okay, give me their names and room numbers sir, so that I can deliver the message."

"You are not getting me," Ifeajuna scratched his head, "we have an urgent message," he screamed. The receptionist was frightened. He did not know that Ifeajuna had lacked a good sleep for the past three days and he was not all by himself, especially after he had just killed Maimalari.

"But sir, give me their names at least," the receptionist said gently.

"Okay. Largema and Ejoor. But I don't know their room numbers."

The receptionist checked through the register and found the names and the room numbers. Although he smelt a rat, he told Ifeajuna and the patched Ezedigbo, who stood at his side with his gun, the room numbers.

"Okay. Do you have master keys for the rooms?" Ifeajuna asked.

*"Master key? I thought they wanted to pass a message,"* he reasoned to himself. "No, sir," he answered.

"Okay. Call Largema's room and tell him he has an urgent message at the reception."

"Sir, there are no telephones in the rooms. They are located at the corridors." The receptionist explained.

"Okay. Lead us to his room then," the Major ordered.

"Sir, I have to be on duty. It's against protocol. I will surely lose my job."

"Your job? Do you want to lose your life?" Ifeajuna cocked his gun and pointed it at him. "I don't have all night. Lead me to the rooms…now."

The receptionist awash with fear came out of the reception box with raised hands and proceeded to the stairs.

"If you make any alarm you will be shot. Understood?" Ifeajuna said as he advanced with him accompanied by Ezedigbo.

"Yes, sir," he nodded.

When they got to the first floor where Largema's room was located, he ordered the hotel receptionist to knock on the door of the Lieutenant-Colonel and to tell him that he was wanted on the telephone.

"Yes?" A voice answered from the inside.

"Room service, sir," the receptionist responded. "There's an urgent message for you on the telephone, sir."

"Okay, I'll be right out."

The telephones were situated in small booths along the corridors. For Largema's Room 115, the telephone booth was only a few steps away. In the meantime, when they heard Largema's voice, Ifeajuna and Ezedigbo, armed with their guns, had stepped back into the corner, from where they would not be detected by the Lieutenant-Colonel when he came out of his room.

Largema came out dressed in his night clothing and yawned as he picked up the receiver which was off the hook.

"Hello, this is Largema. Hello...who is there?"

On hearing his voice and confirming he was the one, the two armed-men came out of the corner and opened fire with their submachine guns. The battalion commander fell down and died instantly.

They carried the body downstairs and proceeded to finish off Ejoor. They burst into many of the rooms but they couldn't find him. An incident that excused him from his room had saved his life. Frustrated, they left for the car with Largema's body and drove off to the Mess. It was 3:50 am.

# 8

# The Perpetual Curse

**Cowards die many times before their deaths; the valiant never taste of death but once.**

William Shakespeare, English poet and playwright.

(April 23, 1564 – April 23, 1616)

*Saturday, January 15, 1966. 3:30 am.*

*Residence of the Premier, Western Region, Ibadan.*

"Throw them into the tonner," Nwobosi ordered his men.

"Yes, sir."

"Captain, Sir, please release me. I have done as promised. I have brought you to the Chief's house," Fani-Kayode who was still tied in the Landrover begged Nwobosi as the Landrover entered the Premier's compound.

"I'm under orders. We won't take any action on you until we get to the HQ in Lagos," the Captain said as he got out of the vehicle.

"You, you, you.Secure those positions," Nwobosi ordered three of soldiers. "You, stay there," he told another. He then proceeded to the centre of the courtyard as he screamed the Premier's name.

"Akintola, come down; you are for lawful arrest by the army on orders from HQ 2 Brigade," Nwobosi shouted.

"Yes, I am coming," a voice from upstairs replied. But there was no movement. Captain Nwobosi reiterated his summons three more times but there was no movement upstairs neither was there any reaction from the Premier. He then fired from his gun at the building but there was no response. When this yielded nothing, the

Captain ordered Second-Lieutenant Egbikor and six other soldiers to follow him into the house and upstairs.

Chief Akintola had just got off the telephone with the wife of his deputy, Chief Remi Fani-Kayode, Adunni, and he was about to dial the number of Lieutenant-Colonel Abogo Largema, the Commanding Officer, 4th Battalion of the Nigerian Army at the Letmauk Barracks, which was not far away from the Premier's Lodge when he heard disturbances at the courtyard. His police guard, which consisted of one Corporal and five constables, had been overpowered by Nwobosi and his men. His generator attendant had also been shot at the back of the head and killed by Nwobosi when the latter had gone into the generator house to put the compound in accustomed darkness. The noise alerted the Premier who had wanted to seek help from the commanding officer of the battalion. Largema and Akintola were good friends. The former had taught the latter how to handle a gun and shoot. Since he was in close proximity to his gun, he picked it up and loaded it with bullets.

*"I'm ready for you,"* he said to himself as he heard approaching footsteps to his bedroom. All other rooms upstairs were unlocked except for the Premier's room. When Nwobosi got to the door and discovered it was locked, he called out the Premier's name and ordered him to come out one last time.

*"Under arrest ke?"* Akintola said to himself, *"Oya, come and greet your mother's husband,"* as he cocked his gun.

When Nwobosi hit the door in an attempt to force it open, the Premier opened fire from inside his bedroom with a submachine gun, shooting contiguously and continuously through the closed door. The first burst immediately wounded one of the soldiers, Gunner Adefi, in the hand. Second-Lieutenant Egbikor was hit in the head while Captain Nwobosi suffered a wound on his left cheek. However, none of the injuries were sufficiently serious to obstruct them. The Captain and his men immediately returned fire as they retreated and descended the stairs. They then left the house in a panic and hid amidst the flowerbeds facing the rear of the building. In the midst of the chaos and cacophonies, two of the soldiers, Lance Bombardier Uloh and Gunner Ajao remained upstairs and hid in one of the other rooms. Chief Akintola, nevertheless, came out of his bedroom which covered the entrance porch, intensified his shooting, and continued to fire at his assailants with his gun without hitting anyone in particular.

"Return fire," Captain Nwobosi ordered his men, which they did, enormously.

"Please sir, surrender sir. Stop shooting, please. They only came to take us to Lagos," Fani-Kayode pleaded and shouted from the Landrover urging the Premier to cease firing and surrender. But the Premier kept on firing until he ran out of ammunition.

Chief Samuel Ladoke Akintola was the 13th *Aare Ona Kakanfo* (Field Marshal General) of Yorubaland. A title, whose holder, according to a widely believed myth, was not expected to live long nor experience a calm death. No man had the temerity to receive this title for seventy-nine years, ever since the last *Kakanfo Aare* Obadoke Latosa of Ibadan died in 1885 during the Kiriji War. Thus, when Akintola was bestowed with the title, it was incumbent on him to die in his prime and gain glory. He was not expected to live a long uninteresting life in oblivion. What gave credence to this title and ensures the generational myth of this perpetual *Aare Ona Kafanfo* Curse was that the recipient possesses excess courage which prevents him from making peaceful resolutions nor knowing when to stop.

"*Krrr, krrr,*" the gun sounded. The Premier had run out of ammunition but the captain and his soldiers did not know this, they thought he was reloading and waiting for them.

Akintola, now powerless, held out a white handkerchief in a sign of surrender and proceeded to the verandah. Ajao and Uloh who had been hiding in one of the other rooms grabbed him by his arms and dragged him downstairs.

"Bring him out, bring him out," Nwobosi shouted repeatedly after the firing had ceased and he sighted his soldiers with the Premier downstairs.

"Now, now, boys. Be gentle. We are friends here," Akintola said resignedly.

"You shot at us. You resisted arrest. It was a direct order from the HQ," Nwobosi thundered, "we are to eliminate anyone who resisted arrest."

"Boys, it is for the good of the country. Why don't we negotiate? I will see to it that you treated well. I have the Prime Minister's ears," Akintola cajoled.

"We are soldiers, sir. We obey direct orders. Egbikor, Chukwu……" Nwobosi called his soldiers and signalled to the two men to open fire on the Premier. Fani-Kayode stared in horror as the Premier endured a deluge of bullets as he fell to his knees still gasping for breath. Nwobosi then joined them in firing at the Premier as he fell backward with a thud as life hurriedly escaped from him. The Captain and his men then released the policemen and proceeded with Fani-Kayode in the Landrover to Lagos as the 3-Ton truck headed towards Abeokuta. They all left Akintola's mutilated body, riddled with bullets, surrounded by empty shell casings soaked in blood, lying there on the bare ground in his courtyard. The *Aare Ona Kakanfo* had fallen to his death. The curse persists.

# 9

# The Beginning of the End

**Things fall apart; the centre cannot hold;**
**Mere anarchy is loosed upon the world.**

William Butler Yeats, Irish poet and playwright.

(June 13, 1865 – January 28, 1939)

*Saturday, January 15, 1966. 3:55 am.*

*Federal Guard's Unit, Dodan barracks, Ikoyi, Lagos.*

"*Hauun…hauun…hauun,*" the general alarm of the Federal Guards' barrack went off. The head of the non-commissioned officers, Regimental Sergeant Major (RSM) Samuel Tayo had ordered the alarms to be sounded. He had been disturbed by vehicular and troop movements up and down the barracks. Also, some gunshots were heard very close to the barracks. As the most senior Warrant Officer and the head of the NCOs, he could not account for two batches of them that had been roused for "internal security operations". He needed answers.

"Everyone, gear up and proceed to your various platoons," Tayo screamed. "One platoon?With me."

But according to the customary military operational system, as NCOs, they needed an officer to give them commands. So, the RSM led his platoon to Major Donatus Okafor's house, their Officer Commanding (OC), at Ikoyi. But he was not in. Okafor had been searching for Brigadier Maimalari who had eluded him and his men by scaling the fence of his house. Confused, they then headed to his deputy's house, Second-Lieutenant Ezedigbo. He was not in too. He was part of the "revolution" arresting the Finance Minister, Chief Festus Okotie-Eboh. Tayo became suspicious when the next in line, Second-Lieutenant Igweze was also not around. So was Lieutenant Joseph Osuma, though he was not part of the mutineers, being a Friday, he had gone to spend the night in a friend's house. Of all the five Federal Guard's officers, only Lieutenant Paul Tarfa, a very junior officer, was at home.

"Sir," the RSM saluted looking rattled, "there is a code red at the barracks, sir."

"What?" Tarfa asked with his eyes wide open as the sleep had escaped them. "Have you contacted the OC?"

"He's not around sir. So is his deputy and the next and the next. That's why we are here sir." Tarfa returned inside, geared up in his combat outfit and proceeded to lead the men.

"We have never experienced a code red in the barracks before, sir, so no one knew the standard procedure nor how to respond," Tayo explained further.

"That's fine RSM, let us go to the barracks," Tarfa said as they proceeded in the RSM's convoy to the Federal Guards' barracks.

"Sir…" a Sergeant saluted the Lieutenant as he alighted from his vehicle on getting to the barracks.

"What's the situation?" Tarfa asked facing the RSM.

"Around 0210 hours some of the NCOs were roused for an IS operation. Forty minutes later another batch of these soldiers was also rolled out. But we did not receive any signal from the 2 Brigade nor from the 2nd Battalion at Ikeja," Tayo explained, "and as the head of the NCOs, I was not briefed by the officers who led these men."

"Any news from the OC? Has anyone seen him?" Tarfa asked the RSM and another Warrant Officer who stood facing him.

"No, sir. When I woke up to the sounds of vehicular movements, I was unperturbed at first. But when sounds of gunshots were heard close to the barracks, I had no choice but to sound the alarm as no officer was around to give orders, sir."

"Did you try the phone lines to call anyone of us?"

"Yes, we did, sir. But all the lines are down. That was why we had to come to your residence, sir."

Yes, all the telephone lines were down. The RSM was correct. After Ifeajuna's address and the distribution of arms and ammunition at the HQ 2 Brigade, Major Ademoyega was tasked with disrupting communications for that night in order for the operation to go on smoothly. He ordered Second-Lieutenants Okocha and Anyafulu to the Post and Telecommunications (P&T) Telephone Exchange to wait there until he joined them, while he went to the Lion Building, the headquarters of the Nigeria Police on Campbell Street in Lagos, around 2:20 am. Driven by Lance-Corporal Umoru, Ademoyega ordered Captain

Adeleke, Second-Lieutenants Wokocha and Nweke, and nine NCOs to accompany him.

On getting there, Major Ademoyega spoke to the police officer in charge and ordered him to stop receiving or transmitting all messages. He told Nweke to see to it that his orders were obeyed. Nweke then posted his men in strategic positions to prevent anyone from entering or leaving the building and remained inside the building to ensure that no messages were received or transmitted. Ademoyega and Adeleke then drove away. These events partially obstructed communications for that night but when the time for action came, the RSM did it the conventional way.

"Okay, gentlemen. Heads up!" Tarfa shouted. "We have to assume that anyone not present here is a hostile. We need a sort of code or password to identify ourselves within the barracks."

"Yes, sir," the soldiers chorused.

"RSM?" Tarfa beckoned and he whispered into his ears.

"Alright everyone, listen up," Tayo roared. "The calling code is "Red" and you respond "Wine". Did we all get that?"

"Yes, sir," they chorused.

When Okafor heard that Brigadier Maimalari had been killed, he was relieved to hear the news and ordered Captain Oji with four NCOs to proceed to the Airport

Junction in Ikeja to check the situation there. They were expecting Obienu's firepower from Abeokuta. Okafor then ordered the remaining soldiers to proceed to the Mess for further instructions. Instead, they disobeyed, passed the Mess to the barracks where they met Tarfa and explained everything to him. The Lieutenant then put the Federal Guards on a protective mood. He gave orders that lookouts and machine guns to be posted around the walls. When Okafor returned to the barracks to arouse more troops for the "revolution", he was shot at and he fled for his life. His soldiers had countermanded his orders to return to the Mess. Instead, they went to the barracks to obey the call of duty. For Okafor, it was a mutiny within a mutiny. A justified mutiny, this time. The Major then went to inform his fellow mutineers that he had just lost his command; the Federal Guards were no longer responding to his orders and had rebelled against him. In fact, they almost killed him when he went back to the barracks to mobilise more troops. It was the beginning of the end for them. The weather got harsher. It was 4:15 am.

"Halt! Who goes there?" the RSM challenged a figure that was coming from the dark.

"A partner," he responded.

"Advance to be recognized," the RSM barked and called out, "Red!"

But the figure did not respond and continued to move towards the RSM. Tayo called out again, "Red!" But there was no response. This time, the RSM cocked his gun and stood at alert in a defensive position with his finger on the trigger and for the third and last time he called out, "Red!" But the figure kept advancing without giving any response. He had forgotten the password and the RSM concluded he was an enemy. With just three shots, the figure dropped dead in a heartbeat. It was collateral damage. A price paid for forgetfulness.

"Donatus, it is your fault," Ifeajuna cried.

"How?" Major Okafor asked, looking confused.

"Are you asking me? You were supposed to take out the GOC. I'm sure he was the one that alerted the barracks. That's why you lost your command. That's why your soldiers had the audacity to shoot at you. Why? They got higher orders," Ifeajuna lamented.

"And I was detailed to take out Maimalari too? Ironsi commanded no troops. He's an administrative general. The Brigadier was the main target. Unfortunately, we wasted much time."

"Really? I did that job for you. If you…."

"Are we going to think of the next line of action or stay here arguing until we get caught?" Ademoyega interrupted.

"We can still regain supremacy if we can connect with Obienu's unit at the Airport junction," Anuforo suggested.

"Yes. I agree with Chris," Ademoyega said, "the Mess is no longer safe for us."

"Okay. But not to arouse suspicion, Donatus and I will move first," Ifeajuna said as he looked worn out. "For contingency, if the airport junction is unsafe, as Ironsi is already against us, let us meet at this place. It is along Abeokuta road," Ifeajuna proceeded to describe the meeting point for them.

All the four corpses on the ground, Maimalari, Mohammed, Pam, and Unegbe, were quickly loaded into the 3-Ton truck including the Finance Minister who was still alive and nervous. The Prime Minister, the wounded Ezedigbo and Largema's corpse, tucked in the car's boot, were still in Ifeajuna's Mercedes Benz which led the exit towards the airport junction as the other vehicles, Anuforo's Peugeot 403, Ademoyega's Landrover, and the 3-Ton truck, followed behind some minutes after they had left. However, Ifeajuna vacillated, presumed the coup had failed, "betrayed" his fellow mutineers and proceeded to the Yaba Military Hospital where he dropped off the injured Ezedigbo as he and Okafor then proceeded towards the Abeokuta road.

Some few kilometers to their rendezvous, the Prime Minister became restless and was muttering to himself as he rattled his prayer beads. Okafor hinted Ifeajuna of the situation who quickly slammed the brakes and came out of the car.

"Are you alright, sir?" Ifeajuna asked the Prime Minister as he opened the side door. "Or would you like some fresh air?"

To Tafawa Balewa, it was a rhetorical question and the decision to answer or not rested on him. Without answering the Major, he gently alighted from the car and ambled towards the darkness as Ifeajuna watched anxiously, oblivious of what the Prime Minister was up to. Then from a slow walk, to a pace and a sprint, the Prime Minister dashed for the darkness. Ifeajuna did not bother to pursue. Quickly, he grabbed his gun from the car, cocked it, and aimed for the fleeing Prime Minister whose white outfit contrasted the darkness and conspicuously gave him away. The "revolution" had failed and the Prime Minister had become a liability to their movement anyway. The Major shot sporadically at the fleeing figure sending the tranquility of the darkness to a bustle of gunfire like the crackle of burning dried leaves. Tafawa Balewa fell as Ifeajuna stared in horror at the darkness as he proceeded to check on his target. The Golden Voice of Africa had been silenced. Quickly, the major moved towards the still body of the Prime Minister and after confirming he was dead, dragged him to a tree trunk, rested the body in a seating position with his clothing still intact, and saluted the dead Prime Minister. Then he and Okafor brought out Largema's corpse from the boot of the car and laid it down beside

Tafawa Balewa's body. Having realised the coup had failed on their part, they sped, en route Abeokuta-Sagamu, towards Enugu in the East, which was nearly 450 kilometres away.

Major Anuforo with his little convoy which comprised of the Landrover and the 3-Ton truck had moved off the Mess with Anuforo leading in his Peugeot. They had gone to the airport junction as initially agreed but when they could not find Ifeajuna they left for the planned rendezvous along the Abeokuta road. At a given point, Major Anuforo sighted Tafawa Balewa's corpse in a sitting position and stopped the convoy. Then he, Second-Lieutenant Igweze, and Major Ademoyega left their vehicles. It then dawned on them that Ifeajuna had "deserted" them having seen the Prime Minister's and Largema's body. Major Anuforo then ordered the soldiers in the truck that the four corpses be dropped off onto the roadside. The bodies were then carried into the bush on the left-hand side of the road by the soldiers. While they were unloading the bodies, Anuforo observed that Okotie-Eboh was still alive and seated in the truck.

"Who is that man?" He asked Ademoyega. But the Finance Minister replied, "I am Okotie-Eboh."

"He controls the treasury and the wealth of the public. Actually, controlled is the word now," Ademoyega added mockingly.

"You can come down, sir," Anuforo ordered the Minister as he stretched his hand towards him. The minister grabbed his hand as he stepped down from the truck.

"Oh! Thank you, thank you," Okotie-Eboh said looking relieved as he descended the step ladder of the truck.

"You are to be shot, sir," the Major told him with a sneer on his face.

"Ha! Please, don't do this," Okotie-Eboh pleaded for his life. "I'll give you anything you want."

"The only thing I want right now is for you to say your last prayers."

"Please, you don't have to do this. I'm begging you."

"I'm sorry, sir. I'm only acting under orders. You are to be shot."

"Please, don't do this," Okotie-Eboh kept on pleading as he was being pushed to the bush by Anuforo and Ademoyega, followed by Igweze and one of the soldiers, to the spot where the bodies of the four senior officers had been dumped.

"Are you going to say your last prayers or not?" Anuforo asked the Minister for the last time but Okotie-Eboh kept on pleading.

When they got to where the corpses were, the Major, without hesitation, with a short burst from his SMG, killed the Finance Minister. Okotie-Eboh's corpse was dumped together with the other corpses in the bush by the roadside. Then, they drove off to the 2nd Recce Squadron in Abeokuta leaving Igweze and three other soldiers on guard over the bodies.

The "revolution" which looked promising at first, was now falling apart like a pack of cards. They had anticipated resistance from loyal troops to the government but it happened too fast and quickly. Things were falling apart for them and their centre did collapse when Ifeajuna and Okafor left for Enugu without informing the others. It was 5:00 am and the cocks all over Lagos had started crowing.

# 10

# The Call of Duty

**The man dies in all who keep silent in the face of tyranny.**

Wole Soyinka, Nigerian novelist, playwright, poet,and lecturer.

(b.July 13, 1934)

*Saturday, January 15, 1966. 5:00 am.*

*Army Cantonment, Ikeja, Lagos.*

"You, you, you, don't just stand there, move the vehicles," the Captain shouted. "What in the heavens are you waiting for? Or do you want me to shoot your rickety legs? Move, move, move," he kept on screaming.

"Captain, what in God's name is going on here? Why the confusion?"

"Morn sir," the Captain saluted, "orders from battalion HQ, sir."

"What is going on? Who gave orders without my consent?" Lieutenant-Colonel Yakubu Gowon asked with a confused look.

"The GOC sir. There's been some sort of disturbance in Lagos."

"Disturbance?"

"Yes sir. The GOC said something more of a mutiny, a coup."

"A coup?"

"The bugle was sounded and all the soldiers were ordered to report to their companies. I got here as fast as I could," Captain Martin Adamu said exasperatedly, unhappy with the barrage of questions directed at him in the course of carrying out his duties, especially so early in the morning.

"Calm down Captain and get me a vehicle," Gowon said as he went inside to gear up.

Lieutenant-Colonel Yakubu "Jack" Gowon had just returned to the country on the morning of Thursday, January 13, 1966, from a top Joint-Service Course in the United Kingdom. As the course drew to a close, the Army Headquarters informed him of his new position as the commander of the 2nd Battalion, Ikeja. His predecessor Lieutenant-Colonel Hillary Njoku had been reassigned to the Nigeria Military Training College (NMTC), in Kaduna. He was supposed to vacate his official quarters on January 16. Ifeajuna, who had sent an officer to pick up Gowon, then offered him a reservation at the luxurious Ikoyi Hotel pending the time Njoku left his residence. But Gowon declined the offer and decided to stay with his friend and namesake, Lieutenant-Colonel James Yakubu Pam, for three days and to catch up on what he had missed in the military and about the country, at 8, Ikoyi Crescent, Ikoyi, which was his official residence when he was the Adjutant-General of the Army Headquarters before he left for England in May 1965. Pam and Gowon were both from the Middle-Belt region, although Gowon was Angas while Pam was Birom. Pam was the first officer in the Army from the Middle Belt. He was of the aristocracy being the son of a Chief of Jos. Pam advised Gowon that since he would soon take over as the Commanding Officer of the 2nd Battalion, he should rather be close to

Ikeja and not be in Ikoyi. Had Gowon agreed to lodge at the Ikoyi Hotel on Ifeajuna's invitation, he would have been killed like Lieutenant-Colonel Abogo Largema. Had he stayed the night with Pam, he would have been arrested, led out, shot, and executed like Pam.

On the morning of Friday the 14th of January, Gowon went to the Brigade Headquarters in Apapa to see Brigadier Zakariya Maimalari, the head of the brigade under whose command he was to serve. Largema, the Commanding Officer of the 4th Battalion, Ibadan, was also there attending the Brigade Training Conference. Maimalari then officially welcomed Gowon to the Brigade and told him of the cocktail party to be held at his residence that night. Gowon declined at first but later consented after much coaxing by the Brigadier. After the cocktail party, Gowon left for Ikeja Cantonment, as Pam had advised, to rest his head for the night until Captain Martin Adamu's voice, barking out orders, woke him up from his tranquil sleep.

"Adamu, where is my transportation?" Gowon shouted at the Captain after he had geared up in his combat dress with a helmet on his head and a service pistol in his right hand. Adamu looked about frenetically and then screamed," Lieutenant Buhari, where is the damn Landrover?"

"On its way sir, sorry sir," a young, tall, lanky officer came trotting towards Gowon and Adamu, "but the tonners are ready. We are waiting for your orders to proceed," Buhari said gasping for breath.

"Get me the Landrover," Adamu roared, "we report to the Commanding Officer now," as he returned Buhari's salute. The 23-year-old Lieutenant returned a few minutes later with the Landrover and with the 3-tonners proceeded to the Battalion Headquarters at Ikeja.

"Here, here and here, we'll set up defence," the officer said pointing to a map of the Lagos Island. "The barracks are secured as we speak but we do not know what they may be planning next."

"Have you contacted the cantonment for more firearms?"

"Yes, sir. They should be here at any moment from now."

"Okay. Let's go over the routine again," the other senior officer said sipping his tea.

"Okay, sir. If we can cut off…."

They were interrupted by Gowon and his men who had just arrived the conference room of the Battalion HQ. He had found the GOC, Aguiyi-Ironsi, the erstwhile Commanding Officer of the Battalion who was to hand over to him that day, Lieutenant-Colonel Hillary Njoku, captains, company commanders, and the battalion hierarchy all crowded together over a map. Njoku was jotting down some figures while Aguiyi-Ironsi, with Charlie, his crocodile carved swagger stick, was sipping his tea.

"Sir," Gowon saluted the GOC, "I got here as quickly as I could. What's with this news I just heard. Can you bring me up to speed?"

Ironsi dropped his teacup and said with a concerned look, "Jack, I don't think there's much time for a short story here. But what is at stake now is that some unknown soldiers are creating trouble in Lagos."

"What kind of trouble sir?"

"That's what we know for now," Njoku interjected.

"Have you contacted the senior officers in Lagos?" Gowon asked sternly, facing the GOC, "Brigadier Maimalari and Colonel Mohammed?"

"No," the GOC replied.

Gowon was surprised and wondered why he was not summoned in the first place. In the military hierarchy, in a situation like this, for Ironsi, as the General Officer Commanding of the Nigerian Army, the first point of contact for orders on military action would be the Commander of the 2nd Brigade headquartered in Apapa, in this case, Brigadier Maimalari, who in turn would arouse the Federal Guards, the combat force directly reachable to him in Lagos. If the situation got worse and more infantry reinforcement was needed, the next unit to draw from would be the 2nd Battalion in Ikeja, then the 4th Battalion in Ibadan. Also, the 2nd Field Battery and 2nd Recce Squadron in Abeokuta would be mustered if mechanised and artillery support were needed to boost combat strength. Surprisingly to Gowon, Ironsi skipped all these steps and didn't summon any of the commanders. Not even Njoku. But he jumped seven ranks below him giving orders to a Lieutenant. Although as the GOC, Ironsi was the only soldier who had the right to enter into any army building in the country. But it was not a normal night and what was necessary was that the situation was kept under control and the rebels arrested.

"However, I have ordered for a formation of a platoon to be led by Lieutenant Walbe for reconnaissance while the companies prepare for combat action," Ironsi added, raising his tone with the stature of a man in charge of a turbulent situation.

"When will they be ready?" Gowon asked.

"What?"

"The platoon sir. When will the men be ready?"

"Oh! When will they be ready?" Ironsi repeated the question as he faced Walbe, the platoon commander.

"Given the nature of the situation and prep time for the soldiers, in three hours, sir. Two and a half hours at the least," Walbe said with his chest out.

"Two and a half hours?" Gowon screamed. He then asked the GOC when the disturbance was first reported. "About 3 o'clock," Ironsi replied. "What time is it now?"

Gowon asked his commanders. "5:35 sir," Major Henry Igboba, Njoku's second-in-command, replied.

"These men have had nearly three hours' advantage," Gowon said facing the GOC, "must we give them the same time again to enable them to reinforce?"

But Ironsi had no clue to his question, neither did he answer him. He just stared at Gowon as he took up his cup and resumed sipping his tea.

"I give everyone fifteen minutes to get ready," Gowon said as he faced the platoon commanders, "Adamu, hasten up Walbe and let's go get these bastards."

The first place Gowon led the response force to was the Prime Minister's residence at Onikan. It was already six o'clock in the morning and Muslim members of the Prime Minister's residence had just finished their pre-dawn meal. It was the Ramadan season. At the residence, Gowon met the Acting Minister for Defence, Alhaji Ibrahim Tanko Galadima, who told him some armed soldiers had kidnapped the Prime Minister. Galadima then left for Ikoyi to inform the other ministers, mostly of his political party, the Northern Peoples' Congress, NPC. Gowon then conducted an exhaustive search of the residence. He found none of the mutineers, no trace, and no clues. He then led his men to the parliamentary buildings where the office of the Prime Minister was. Again, he found no evidence. Then he went to the Federal Guards' barracks that was responsible for the safety of service officers and government officials. There, Gowon met Lieutenant

Paul Tarfa and the RSM Samuel Tayo who briefed him and brought him up to speed about the situation and how their Officer Commanding and his two deputies had gone missing. It was in the middle of this briefing that Captain Emmanuel Nwobosi and his contingents arrived with their hostage, Fani-Kayode. The Mess had been the rallying point for all the mutineers but Nwobosi did not know that their "revolution" had collapsed and Ifeajuna who had ordered him to Ibadan had fled with Okafor to Enugu. They had discouraged any mode of electronic communication because they could be easily picked up by the Special Branch of the Police Operations Command and the Army Signals.

"Sir," a Sergeant came running in and saluted Gowon, "some unidentifiable soldiers just arrived in a Landrover and a 3-tonner. They are presently in the compoundsir and it looks like they've got a hostage with them."

Quickly, Gowon ordered that the Mess be secured, put on a defensive guard, and rounded up with soldiers. He then proceeded to the verandah and called out over a megaphone for Nwobosi to surrender.

"This is Lieutenant-Colonel Yakubu Gowon of the Nigerian Army. You are completely surrounded. Drop your weapons and surrender."

Nwobosi himself had wondered whether they were reporting too early or too late at the time he got to the Mess when he could not find any of the other renegade units. What made it worse was that all the soldiers wore the same uniforms, so he could not figure out who was with them or against them. As soon as he heard Gowon's voice, he knew he had entered a trap, a holy trap nonetheless, because if it were up to Tarfa, there would have been a bloody fight because he had suggested that grenades should be launched at them giving them no chance to surrender. But Gowon, always the diplomat, applied caution, overruled Tarfa, and opined that the hostage could be the Prime Minister and wouldn't want any harm done to him. When Nwobosi discovered he had been truly surrounded. He quickly destroyed the paper, on which the written instructions about how the coup would go, Ifeajuna gave to him and brought out the signal Ifeajuna had forged in Maimalari's name authorising their actions.

"Who's the hostage in the truck?" Gowon asked as he approached Nwobosi.

"The deputy premier of the Western Region," Nwobosi replied.

"Fani Power?"

"Yes, sir,"

"Where's the Prime Minister? Do you know anything about his whereabouts?" Gowon asked.

"No, sir. Our unit was detailed to proceed to Ibadan and arrest the Premier and his deputy. We know nothing about the Prime Minister."

"Where then is the Premier?"

"He's dead. He resisted arrest. We were acting under orders sir," Nwobosi said as he proceeded to show Gowon the signal Ifeajuna gave him.

"This is a forged signal," Gowon said as he read it. "You just committed a treasonable offence punishable under death."

"We were following orders, sir. We are soldiers, sir," Nwobosi protested.

"Yeah, right," Gowon scoffed. "Boys," Gowon screamed at RSM Tayo and his platoon members, "round them up and secure them in the guardroom." He then peeped into the Landrover which still had the tied Fani-Kayode.

"You are safe now, sir. Everything is under control," Gowon assured him and called out to Tarfa. "Lieutenant, see to it that our guest is safe and treated well." As he proceeded to leave, he tapped Tarfa on the shoulder and said,

"I must commend you and the RSM for your professionalism and a job well done. Keep it up and…you are still in command here."

Gowon and his force then left, after he had been sure the barracks was safe enough and in the hands of men he could trust, for the Ikoyi residences of the senior officers. All of whom had been killed except for Aguiyi-Ironsi who was still at Ikeja sipping his tea and barking out orders. It was 6:45 am and the day was now breaking all over Lagos.

# 11

# Sheep without Shepherd

**I asked for soldiers, I'm being given politicians dressed in uniforms.**

Major-General Johnson Thomas Umunakwe Aguiyi-Ironsi, Nigerian general and first military Head-of-State.

(March 3, 1924 – July 29, 1966)

### *Saturday, January 15, 1966. 7:00 am.*

### *Ikoyi Hotel, Ikoyi, Lagos.*

"*Gbam, gbam, gbam.*"

"Who for God's sake bangs my door this early morning?" A voice roared from inside the hotel room.

"*Oga!* Open the door. *Trouble don dey oo…plenty, plenty palava.*"

"What the…." Lieutenant-Colonel David Ejoor stopped in the middle of his words as he noticed it was his driver who had been banging the door. "But I told you to get enough rest. I don't want you sleeping on the wheels while driving me to Enugu."

"*Oga, no be like that. Na the Prime Minister some soja men carry go. In fact, I bin hear say dem don even kill some of their oga dem. Blood just full everywhere.*"

"What? Blood? Are you sure of what you are saying? I hope you are not drunk this early morning?" Ejoor asked with a surprised look.

"*I sure, saa. Na Apapa I sleep over. Na soso up and down wakawaka some soja men dey do since 3 o'clock. When I hear say dem come dis hotel, na hin muy heart commot for my bodi, na so I take rush down hia. Oga, true…true…I no lie.*"

"Yes! I now believe that you are drunk," Ejoor said nodding his head.

*"Haba, Oga! For this early momo, I neva drink anything…not even water. Na the truth be dat."*

While Ejoor was still waiving off his driver contending he was drunk, Largema's driver came rushing in and showed the men bullet casings he found in front of his superior's hotel room. The three men then went to Largema's room upstairs to find traces of blood that had congealed on the corridor due to the harmattan and the telephone hook that was still dangling. Dazed, flustered, and fluttered, Ejoor staggered back to his room, changed into his military kit and directed his driver to 8, Ikoyi Crescent, Ikoyi, Lagos, the home of the Adjutant-General, the officer who handled the death of soldiers in the army, to take some of the blood samples to really determine whether it was Largerma who had been murdered in cold blood. Ejoor was still skeptical of the events he just found himself in. He wanted answers.

"Who could have had the audacity to murder a commander of a whole battalion?" He thought to himself as his driver approached the residence of Lieutenant-Colonel James Yakubu Pam.

"Uncle Jack!" Kaneng screamed as she heard Ejoor knocked at the door.

She had thought it was Gowon who had come earlier to assure them he would bring their father back to them. But as she opened the door, she stared hard at the unfamiliar face and then screamed, "Mummy". The 30-year-old Mrs. Elizabeth Pam hurriedly came downstairs.

She was tending to her twins who had been restless since their father was taken away by Major Chukwuka and his men. She herself had cried her eyes out but hanged on to his promise that he would return to her and the children. When she saw Ejoor, she assumed he would have more information about her husband since he was a senior officer like Gowon.

"Good morning."

"Morning Ma'am," Ejoor replied courteously.

"Kaneng go upstairs and look after your young ones," Elizabeth said to her eldest daughter and she ushered Ejoor in.

"Any news about my husband?" Elizabeth asked as they took their seats. Ejoor looked more surprised.

"Sorry, my manners. Would you like to take some water?"

"No, no, no," Ejoor answered looking more troubled. "I came looking for your husband. Is anything the matter? Where is he? What's wrong? What's going on?"

Elizabeth was confused as well, but she answered his inundating questions anyway. "Humphrey and some soldiers came for him around 2 o'clock this morning. They said he was needed at the office." She then asked him after a pause, "Did Jack not tell you anything?"

"Gowon?"

"Yes. He was here nearly an hour ago. He promised he would return with my husband as soon as necessary. But I have a terrible feeling."

Elizabeth then went on to narrate to Ejoor how around 2 am they noticed crawling soldiers led by her husband's deputy, Major Chukwuka, whom she knew very well, approached their house, climbed the telecom pole and scaled their fence. They were trying to avoid the guards which they later caught and arrested. They shot at the two front tyres of her husband's official car and at the kitchen door to forcefully gain entry. She said they were so terrified that they knew it was an ominous situation.

As she recounted her side of the story, Ejoor listened with rapt attention. He did not inform her nor let her know of Largema's blood at the Ikoyi hotel. His doubts were now eluding him. He assured her that her husband would be found and brought home safe and sound. He then left for Brigadier Maimalari's residence but found no one there with the place deserted. Finally, he left for the GOC's house where he met his absence. However, he met his wife, Mrs. Victoria Aguiyi-Ironsi who told him Gowon had come to check on the house and had told her, her husband was at the 2nd Battalion Headquarters in Ikeja issuing out orders. At once, Ejoor, still looking for concrete answers, ordered his driver to proceed to Ikeja. It was a Saturday morning and residents of Lagos, Abeokuta, and Ibadan were already waking up to another adventurous weekend oblivious of what had happened in the course of the cold, starless, and bloody night.

"Morn'g sir," Ejoor saluted the GOC on sighting him as he entered the Battalion HQ conference room. Ironsi who had his back to Ejoor, turned and on seeing him quickly drew out his pistol and pointed it at him.

"Ha! David, who sent you to kill me?"

Ejoor was stunned but he subtly replied, "No one, sir. Why would I kill you?"

The GOC stared at him for a moment, read his body language, and then holstered his weapon.

"I'm sorry I had to react that way. The events of the past few hours have taken a toll on me. I don't know who to trust. In fact, I do not trust any officer right now"

"It's alright, sir. That's why I'm here. But first of all, I need to know what is really going on? Largema is dead, Pam is unaccounted for and I found the Brigadier's residence deserted. I then went over to your house but Madam directed me here. Sir, what's going on?" Ejoor asked with a confused look.

"Largema is dead?" Ironsi asked as he sank into a chair.

"Affirmative, sir. He was murdered in front of his room. I saw it myself."

"How did you know that David?" Ironsi suddenly stood up and towered above the young officer who did not flinch at all.

"We lodged at the same hotel, sir."

"How then, did you escape?" Ironsi asked with a suspicious look.

"I didn't, sir. I never encountered the killers. I never knew until this morning when my driver came banging at my door. I changed my hotel room. So, they must have missed me if I was their target in the first place," Ejoor answered boldly.

Ejoor was right. As the Commanding Officer of the 1st Battalion in Enugu, he had received a signal in the name of Brigadier Zakariya Maimalari on the 9th of January that he had been invited to a three-day Brigade Training Conference on the 12th to 14th January, in Apapa, Lagos. On the 10th of January, Ejoor left for Lagos and was booked into room 17 of the Ikoyi Hotel. However, when he returned from the day's programme on the 13th of January, the air conditioning system had been left on all day which caused the room to be extremely cold. He then opened the windows to thaw the coldness of the room after he had changed into his nightwear only to discover his privacy could be easily seen by anyone in the adjacent buildings. He loved his privacy and would not like to encounter prying eyes. The following morning, he asked for a change of room at the reception. After the conference training of 14th January, he went to Maimalari's residence for the cocktail at 7:30 pm and had planned to leave around 9:00 pm because he had to return to Enugu by road the next day but he left around 11:00 pm. The next morning, he woke up to his driver banging on his door.

"Well," Ironsi sighed, "some junior officers are causing trouble all over Lagos. I got to know when domestic staff at the Prime Minister's residence called me around three o'clock that some officers had come to take him away and I immediately suspected it was a mutiny. At once, I geared up and came here to Ikeja to rouse the soldiers to arrest the situation and bring the rebels to book."

"Have you heard from Enugu, sir?"

"Enugu? Our main concern here is to rid Lagos of these troublemakers before things spiral out of control." Ironsi clenched his teeth.

"It's alright, sir. Since you have enough hands here already, I would love to proceed to Enugu by the fastest means possible to provide help from the Eastern corridor," Ejoor said calmly.

"Well, I cannot order you to Enugu now. I need you here," Ironsi countered.

"But sir, I have to be in command of my battalion at this crucial time."

"Hmm. David, are you with me or against me?" Ironsi queried.

Ejoor replied, "You are my commanding officer, sir, you know whatever it is I'm always with you."

"Then stay with me."

"I wish I could, sir," Ejoor enthused, "but military code requires that in time of a crisis, a commander must connect with his unit and take charge."

"Are you lecturing me on military ethics now, David? Stay! That's a direct order."

"Actually, sir," Ejoor coaxed, "I'm acting on your orders. The signal you signed that was distributed to us by Brigadier Maimalari at the Brigade Training Conference stated that *Commanders should tighten security when they get back to their units and to warn all their subordinates against disloyal acts*. That is why I have to be in Enugu."

"Alright," Ironsi said resignedly, "but keep me apprised of any developments."

Ejoor saluted and made to leave. He then looked for Igboba and ordered him to clear a security flight to Enugu through the airport commandant. A few hours later, Ejoor was at the airport on his way to Enugu.

"Sir," Major Igboba called the attention of the GOC after he had escorted Ejoor out of the Headquarters, "Mr. Marsden, Mr. Duckett, and Mr. Maiduguri are here to see you, sir. They said it's urgent."

"Show them in," Ironsi, who was having a discussion with Njoku in the conference room, said.

"DIG, ASP, CP," Ironsi greeted the police officers as he warmly shook their hands.

"General," Marsden said after he had released Ironsi's hand, "we have been ordered by the Council of Ministers to bring you in for a situational report immediately."

"Council of Ministers?" Ironsi asked with a surprised look.

"Yes, sir," Marsden responded, "the helicopter is waiting outside. I'll fill you in on transit. But right now, we have to move."

"Okay. Hillary," the GOC called out to Njoku, "let's go. Igboba, you are in command here. You know how to reach me," Ironsi said as he took Charlie, his crocodile carved swagger stick.

"Alright, gentlemen. We're ready," Ironsi signalled as the British police officers led the way to the helicopter.

Around 5:30 am, the Minister for Works, Alhaji Shehu Shagari, a devout Muslim who had just eaten his predawn meals and finished his prayers in his Ikoyi residence as the Ramadan period required, was alerted by a civil servant in the Ministry of Defence that the Prime Minister had been abducted under gunpoint by unknown soldiers. Immediately, the Minister tried to get across to the Sardauna and Premier of the Northern Region in Kaduna but the phone lines were down. Looking ruffled, Shagari quickly informed his next-door neighbour, the Minister for Housing and Surveys, Chief Adeniran Ogunsanya. After he had relayed his message to him, he then left to alert the Minister of Transport,

Zanna Bukur Dipcharima, who quickly summoned other cabinet members of the NPC who then converged at his home in Bourdillon Road, Ikoyi.

By 7:00 am, most of the NPC ministers had assembled at Dipcharima's house. When the Acting Minister of Defence, Ibrahim Tanko Galadima told them Okotie-Eboh had been kidnapped as well, they became confused than shocked. He also added that not the whole army but ạ rebellious unit was responsible and that Aguiyi-Ironsi was in Ikeja issuing orders. While they were still pondering over who could have abducted Tafawa Balewa and Okotie-Eboh, news came in that Akintola was dead and his body had been found riddled with bullets and the Sardauna too had been gunned down in Kaduna with his house razed to the ground. The information added that the coup plotters were organising from the North to kill them too. At that point, a real fear crushed their minds and they heaved and sighed as they gasped for their breath. Without wasting time, Dipcharima hurried to his neighbour, Donald Frederick Hawley, the British Deputy High Commissioner and requested him to send for his superior, Francis Cumming-Bruce, the British High Commissioner, for an urgent meeting. Dipcharima, who has been acting as Prime Minister as the most senior NPC politician in the cabinet, then ordered the Police to bring in Ironsi for an evaluation and a way-forward meeting. The Acting Deputy Inspector General of Police, Leslie Marsden, the Assistant Superintendent of Police, George Duckett, and the Lagos Commissioner of Police, Hamman Maiduguri then left by helicopter to Ikeja to fetch the GOC. The Acting Inspector General of Police, Alhaji Kam Selem, was also called upon for the meeting.

"Ambassador, thanks for coming on such a short notice," Dipcharima got up to shake the hands of the diplomat as soon as he entered his living room.

"It's my pleasure. My deputy has given me a summary of the situation," FCB said as he took his seat.

"Yes, thank you. My colleagues and I have decided to seek your country's assistance at this time. We never envisaged what happened this morning and we didn't anticipate how to respond to it at this time," Dipcharima said calmly.

"Okay, I'm all ears."

"Our fear is that the army could break down and total anarchy could let loose among the military circle. We are also suspicious of the GOC's actions ever since we got wind of the situation. But we feel with the presence of your country's armed forces, it would dispel the rebels here in Lagos and dampen the resolve of the rebels up North who had promised to march down to the South to annihilate all of us," Dipcharima continued.

"Well," FCB replied, "since this is a request from a sovereign country to another sovereign country. It is advisedly necessary that the request is written down if we are to concur at all and to be signed by the constitutionally approved authority."

Constitutionally approved authority? The ministers looked at one another and exchanged glances. "Who then is the appropriate authority since the whereabouts of the Prime Minister is unknown and there is no Deputy Prime Minister?" They thought to themselves.

Whenever the Prime Minister, Sir Abubakar Tafawa Balewa was not around, the Minister for Defence, Alhaji Muhammadu Ribadu usually acted as the Prime Minister. But he died in on May 1, 1965, and Inua Wada took over as Defence Minister. On the morning the military boys struck, Inua Wada had been out of the country, in London, for an eye operation and Ibrahim Tanko Galadima, the Minister for State for Defence, acted as Defence Minister. Since the portfolio was not substantive on Galadima, the next in line on the power organogram was Dipcharima, the Minister of Transport, as the most senior NPC politician in the Council of Ministers in the absence of Tafawa Balewa and Inua Wada. That was why Dipcharima was chairing the meetings concerning the state of affairs of the nation, he was already coordinating with the security forces, the Police, and the Army, to stop the mutiny and find the abducted.

The GOC and the Acting IGP were then called in to give their reports and the assessment of the whole situation. When they were through with it, they left for the Police Headquarters where they continued their "battle" against the coup plotters who had fled Lagos and some of them arrested.

"Sir, the Attorney-General is here," FCB's secretary interrupted the conversation.

"Elias," Dipcharima called out as the AGF walked in.

"Bukar, is it true?" Elias asked.

Dipcharima nodded in the affirmative. The AGF then broke down and started weeping.

"Come on, we'll find them. They are not dead yet," Dipcharima rebuked him. "Be a man and stop crying. There's no time to show emotions here. We need to take a stand now. It's time for action."

After the AGF had stopped crying and comported himself, the British High Commissioner, his deputy, and his secretary stood up to leave and Dipcharima promised to get back to them once they resolved the leadership issue.

"My colleagues," Dipcharima broke the long silence, "we cannot make a decision without the presence of the NCNC ministers. So, for security reasons and for our own safety, I suggest we hold our meeting at the Police Force HQ. Or what do you think?"

"I agree, but we have already nominated you as the acting Prime Minister," Chief Richard Akinjide, the Minister for Education replied. All the other ministers nodded in approval to Akinjide's words.

"Okay then. But we still have to notify them of the developments. Most importantly, the Acting President will still have to confirm my nomination."Dipcharima affirmed.

So, they all left for the rendezvous while Shagari was detailed to inform the NCNC ministers of the meeting place and to apprise them of the new developments. The ministers had been at the Minister for Trade, Kingsley Ozumba Mbadiwe's residence in Ikoyi holding a caucus meeting and were still there when Shagari arrived and informed them there was going to be an emergency cabinet meeting. Then, like a sheep without a shepherd, they all left for the Police Force Headquarters at Moloney Street. It was 12:00 pm and ten hours since the H-Hour. Yet, there was still no clue on the whereabouts of the Prime Minister and the Finance Minister. Nigeria's First Republic was coming to an end.

## Some Common Terms

ADC – Aide-*de*-Camp.

AG – Action Group, a party in the first Republic led by Chief Obafemi Awolowo (1909–1987).

ASP – Assistant Superintendent of Police.

*Babaringa*- A flowing robe commonly worn by men in Northern Nigeria.

Battalion – Two or more companies.

Battery – a small Artillery military unit commanded by a Major or a senior Captain.

BM – Brigade Major.

*Bokoto* – Peppered cow-leg.

Brigade – Two or more battalions, usually commanded by a Brigadier.

Chief-of-Staff – an officer responsible for coordinating staff matters on behalf of a senior army officer.

CO – Commanding Officer.

Company – means a small infantry

CP – Commissioner of Police.

Coup D'état –an attempted

DAG – Deputy Adjutant-General.

DIG – Deputy Inspector General of Police.

FCB – Francis Cumming-Bruce (1912–2013), British High Commissioner to Nigeria (the equivalent to an Ambassador) during the coup.

GOC – General Officer Commanding.

HQ – Headquarters.

IGP – Inspector General of Police.

IS – Internal Security.

Mutiny – An organised rebellion against a legally constituted authority.

NA – Nigeria Army.

NAE – Nigeria Army Engineers.

NCNC – National Council of Nigerian Citizens, led by Dr. Nnamdi Azikiwe (1904–1996).

NCO – Non-commissioned officer: it refers to all 'other ranks' above Lance Corporal and below Lieutenant.

NMTC – Nigerian Military Training College.

NPC – Northern Peoples' Congress, led bySirAhmadu Bello (1909–1966)

OC – Officer Commanding.

Officers' Mess – A rest and recreation center for the exclusive use of Officers.

P&T – Post and Telecommunications.

Platoon - a military unit that is a subdivision of a company usually commanded by a Lieutenant.

PM – Prime Minister.

Ranks in the Nigerian Army:

Officers

- Field Marshal (No Nigerian military officer has ever attained this rank)
- General
- Lieutenant-General
- Major-General
- Brigadier or Brigadier-General
- Colonel
- Lieutenant-Colonel
- Major
- Captain
- Lieutenant
- Second Lieutenant.

Other Ranks

- Warrant Officer Class 1
- Warrant Officer Class 2
- Staff Sergeant

- Sergeant
- Corporal
- Lance Corporal
- Private.

Other Ranks used as of January 15, 1966.

- Gunner (Private in the Artillery)
- Bombardier (Corporal in the Artillery)
- Lance Bombardier, (Lance Corporal in the Artillery).

RSM – Regimental Sergeant Major: the most senior NCO in a battalion or regiment.

Recce – Reconnaissance.

SMG – Submachine gun.

Troop – means a group of soldiers, corresponding to an infantry company.

Made in United States
North Haven, CT
25 June 2022

20626886R00071